RIMROCK BASIN SHOWDOWN

Matt Curtis inherited Rimrock Basin from his father, but when he arrived to claim the inheritance he found that Lear Holbrook had already grabbed it. Both the town and the neighbouring territory were under this man's control and Matt found himself in a fight to gain possession of his property. When Holbrook sent his men to wipe out Matt and his partners, Matt fought them off, but it was time to face Holbrook at his ranch and finish it once and for all, in a bloody showdown.

RIMROCK BASIN
SHOWDOWN

Rimrock Basin Showdown

by

Paul K. McAfee

Dales Large Print Books
Long Preston, North Yorkshire,
BD23 4ND, England.

British Library Cataloguing in Publication Data.

McAfee, Paul K.
    Rimrock Basin showdown.

    A catalogue record of this book is
    available from the British Library

    ISBN   1-84262-354-0 pbk

First published in Great Britain 2004 by Robert Hale Limited

Copyright © Paul K. McAfee 2004

Cover illustration © Prieto by arrangement with
Norma Editorial S.A.

The right of Paul K. McAfee to be identified as the author of this
work has been asserted by him in accordance with the
Copyright, Designs and Patents Act, 1988

Published in Large Print 2005 by arrangement with
Robert Hale Ltd.

Dales Large Print is an imprint of Library Magna Books Ltd.

Printed and bound in Great Britain by
T.J. (International) Ltd., Cornwall, PL28 8RW

*This book is dedicated to
Shirley, my love, and to
Don and Nancy,
Loved and deeply appreciated*

CHAPTER ONE

Matt Curtis rode his buckskin up to the hitch rail before the building that held a small sign, RIMROCK LAND OFFICE. He dismounted and, looping the reins over the pole, stretched and, taking the makings from a vest pocket, leaned against the rack and lighted a smoke. As he lighted the cigarette, he looked up and down the main street of the town.

Curtis was slightly over six feet, rangy, with the thin hips of a horseman. His shoulders were wide, supporting the deep width of his chest. His eyes, Scots gray-green, were sharp and all seeing, the eyes of a rangeman, needing to note every movement within the limits of his vision. Carried low upon his right thigh, rode a well-worn Colt .44. The weapon had the look of a utilitarian instrument for daily needs, rather than the weapon of a gunman.

Matt stirred himself, finished the smoke and tossed it into the street. He ground out the sparks with his heel. Pushing back his hat he stepped upon the boardwalk and entered the land office.

A half-hour later he left the land office and stood looking about the town. A few buildings down the street he saw a sign indicating that 'Sleep and Eat' were available. He strolled along the boardwalk, taking in the sights of the town about him, and entered the hotel. The dining-room for the establishment was off the lobby on the right as he entered. Odors of food being cooked and served drifted out into the lobby, teasing his nostrils and causing his stomach to growl with hunger. It had been long since dawn when he had dined meagerly upon hard biscuits and jerky, with creek water to down each dry mouthful.

He entered the dining-room and, seeing a table nearby already set with silverware and napkin, he took a seat and placed his hat upon an empty chair across from him. A pretty young woman approached his table and smiled at him.

'Hi. You look hungry. What can I bring you?'

He grinned at her and widened his eyes as he saw how pretty she actually was. Her eyes were sparkling brown, brown hair swept back and caught at her nape with a red ribbon. Her eyebrows were dark and broad, her nose strong and her mouth wide and smiling. No raving beauty, he thought, but she sure is pretty.

'Mister, I'm not on the menu.' Her eyes twinkled at him. A couple at a table across the room heard her sally and laughed. 'Would you like coffee, some roast beef and potatoes? Anyway, that's our special for today.'

He brought himself up out of his thoughts with a start, reddening as he realized what she had said. Then he grinned and nodded.

'All that, and whatever else that goes with it. And end it with about half of that apple pie I smelled as I came through the door.'

She laughed. 'You have a good nose all right. The pies just came out of the oven. Your meal is coming right up, coffee first.' She smiled at him, coloring slightly at his bold, admiring glance and, turning, disappeared into the kitchen. He enjoyed her lithe step and the full swing of her body as she walked away from him. A full-bodied young woman, he thought. Someone surely must be lucky to be her beau.

She brought his coffee quickly and as quickly began serving other customers. It was not until she brought his plate, filled

11

with roast beef, boiled potatoes, carrots and snap beans, that he got another chance to talk with her.

'My name is Matt Curtis,' he told her as she served his meal. 'I just got into town.'

'I knew you were a stranger,' she replied softly. 'You have never been here before to eat. I am Emmy, Emmy Henry. It's nice to see a new face.' She stood back and smiled at him, her eyes taking in his broad shoulders and the laugh wrinkles about his eyes, liking what she saw. 'My father owns the livery at the end of the street. We run the hotel and live in rooms on the second floor.'

A customer called for service and she gave him another quick smile and left, walking self-consciously, sure that his eyes were upon her.

And I'll be back to eat some more of your cooking, and learn if there really is a man in your life, Matt thought, as he watched her move across the room. She became busy with noon customers and he had no further opportunity to chat with her. Unknown to him, however, from time to time she shot a glance across the room at the stranger who had been so friendly and whose smile seemed to make her heart flutter.

The horses came through the sharp pass into the basin, moving briskly along the narrow trail. Matt Curtis headed the herd, moving across the front of it, making certain none of the animals tried to leave the path and move into the trees and brush that lined it. There was little room for them to maneuver, but one never knew what an adventuresome yearling might do.

The herd was trailed by Sam Tracy, Matt's close friend since the Civil War. They had served together under Sherman during his grueling march through Georgia, and up through the Carolinas at the end of the war. Released from the army at the same time, and both being from the Dakota Territory, they decided to come West together.

It had been Matt's long-time dream to develop a horse ranch and raise blooded animals, improving their bloodlines until he would be able to market the best horses possible.

Sam liked the idea and they became partners in the project. The last of the horses dashed past, driven by Sam and Al Rooney, an elderly cowboy of somber turn. Sam drew his horse beside Matt and grinned through mud-splattered features at his partner.

'Well, come what may, partner, we are

here. And I must say, I never saw a purtier place. That there grass must be stirrup-high everywhere you look.'

Matt nodded. 'We've got us a nice place here, Sam. We'll keep the herd down so every animal has as much to graze as the next. We'll sell the best and breed back to the best, in form and color. Before long we'll be selling some of the best horseflesh in the West.'

'I agree with you, Matt. Now, just where did your uncle say that cabin was?'

Matt leaned over and drew a worn envelope from a saddlebag. He drew a heavy sheet of paper from it, well-creased and worn, but showing clear lines. He traced a stream across the center of the page and pointed.

'Right there. We've come in from the south. Rimrock was five miles back. The cabin sits there, at the edge of a bend in the creek.' He raised his head and looked about him. 'I'd say it's over there.' He pointed toward the crest of a rolling slope. 'Over that rise there, and follow the creek until we come to it.'

'Then let's go find it,' said Sam. 'Al can move the horses along some further in. They ain't gonna leave this grass soon. When they've had their fill we can move them further in...'

Matt shook his head. 'No, we had better move them now and get them closer to the cabin. All three of us will ride herd on them tonight. By tomorrow they won't want to leave the grass.'

Sam nodded agreement and rode on, as the three of them hazed the reluctant animals before them, away from the entrance into the basin. The sun was nearing the horizon when they finally drove the herd over the rim and dropped down a long, grassy slope toward a gentle bend in the creek.

Matt paused and looked about him. A stand of aspen and pine stood several hundred yards back of the bend and there, the roof hardly visible, he spied the cabin.

'There it is, boys. Turn 'em loose. They're home and so are we.' There was elation in his voice. Maybe, just maybe this was the real beginning of his dream.

CHAPTER TWO

Lear Holbrook considered Rimrock his town. In his office at the rear of the Rimrock saloon, with his chosen lieutenants about him, he ruled the community. So he thought. If there were pieces of territory he wished to acquire, he did not question. He either bought the land at his own price or drove its owner from it. From time to time a family pulled out of Rimrock, silently, not talking. His threats were all that was needful, in such cases, to cause owners to take a pittance for their possessions and, in fear of Holbrook's men, decide to leave rather than fight.

One piece of property he had his eye on, for good cause in his thinking, was the Rimrock basin, about five miles from the town. In fact, he already considered it his property and instructed the Rimrock land office owner to sign papers giving him the land.

Howie Burkhart, the land office agent, was no friend of Holbrook. He hated the man with a passion. Early in Holbrook's takeover of the town, he had refused to allow Holbrook access to the land office books. Two hours later three of Holbrook's minions arrived. They locked the office and took Burkhart into a back room and proceeded to beat him until he could not stand.

From time to time, on request, Howie Burkhart opened the books to Holbrook. For some reason, however, he had recorded Matt Curtis's claim to Rimrock Basin in another book and had hidden it among his personal belongings in his cabin. He sensed something pending in the face of the young, serious stranger who filed upon the Rimrock basin. Howie knew Holbrook wanted the basin. Why, he did not know. Holbrook had no cattle, no horse-herd. There had been no mining in the basin that Howie had ever heard of. He had spent the night following Matt Curtis's visit to his office pondering the question. Why was Holbrook so interested in the basin?

Holbrook claimed the basin regardless of records and when Jesse Thomas came to his office several weeks after Matt had taken over the basin, he was astounded and disbelieving of what he heard.

'Boss, did you let someone go into the

basin, back there in the mountains? The one you've had your eye on?'

Holbrook dropped the paper he was reading and spun from his desk to confront the informant.

'What did you say?'

'I asked if you had let someone into the basin up there on the edge of the mesa.'

Holbrook glared at him. 'No, I did not! What are you talking about?'

Thomas, foreman for what cattle Holbrook ran on the edge of the mesa, shifted his feet, twisting his hat in his hands.

'Wa'al, there's three guys and a whole bunch of hosses up thar in the basin right now.'

Holbrook's face darkened. He knew he should have filed upon the land long before now, but he had other plans of procurement. He grunted angrily.

'Wonder how come I never heard anything about it until now. Were you up there? Did you see the horses?'

'Yep. I reckon thar's about two hundred or so hosses. An' like I said, I saw only three men.'

Holbrook dismissed the man, flipping him a coin for a drink on his way out of the establishment. The man caught the coin and nodded his thanks, closed the office door and headed for the bar.

The saloon-owner grabbed his hat, left the building through a back entrance and in a few minutes was leaning over the counter at the land office, glaring at Howie Burkhart.

'Let me see the register for the past month,' he growled at the agent.

'Sure thing, Mr Holbrook. You just looked at the books last week, but here they are.' The man shoved the books over to Holbrook.

The town boss grabbed the books with the earliest dates and ran a blunt forefinger down the listings, which were few. He continued to the most current date and then slammed the book closed. Shoving it across to Burkhart he glared at him.

'Are you holding out on me? Is there another book?'

The land agent's heart skipped a beat, but his expression of puzzlement did not change.

'No, sir, Mr Holbrook. You're lookin' at the only listing. It's agin the law to have double books, you know.'

Holbrook glared at him. 'Do you know anything about hosses being run up there in Rimrock basin? I've been told by one of my men that someone has moved onto the land.'

Burkhart shook his head. 'No, sir. I ain't heard anything like that at all.' In his mind the agent could see the spine of the book, with Matt Curtis's filing in it, sitting among other books, on the shelf above his desk in his home.

Holbrook held his gaze for a long moment and then straightened. He pointed a finger directly under Burkhart's nose.

'If you hear of anything like that happening you come and tell me, hear? And keep your mouth shut about what I just told you.' Burkhart jerked his head up and down affirmatively, gulping so his prominent Adam's apple ran up and down his neck.

The burly saloon-owner stomped out of the office, slamming the door back of him. Burkhart gulped and shuddered. But there was a feeling of satisfaction in that the angry bully had not gotten helpful information from him. Matt Curtis's filing, if it was secret, was still intact as ever.

Holbrook leaned back in his chair and lighted a cigar. Through the smoke he squinted at his second in command, Lance Rainey. Rainey sat on a hard, straight chair to one side of the room.

'I want you to send one your gunslicks out to the basin and take care of whoever it is ramrodding that outfit, who's slipped into the place. I'll give a hundred dollars to whoever gets the job done, no questions asked, and no talking about it later.'

Rainey was a tall, amazingly skinny man, with pale features and dead, lusterless eyes. His mouth was a blue slit beneath a sharp, pointed nose. He was Holbrook's shadow. Wherever the saloonkeeper went, Rainey was there. He listened now, as Holbrook spoke to him.

'Someone has slipped into the basin. I want them out. Is that kid still around who was trying so hard to make a few notches on his gun?'

Rainey nodded, his eyes cold and unmoving on the face of his boss.

'He's spending most of his time practicin' his draw.' The thin slit of a mouth twisted wryly. 'Not much good, but he thinks he's among the best.'

Holbrook was silent, looking out of the window of his office. He looked at Rainey again.

'I think I have a job for him. He just might get to file a notch on his gun.'

The third night, following Holbrook's learning of Matt Curtis's presence in the Rimrock basin, the three men gathered about their camp-fire on a flat space between the old cabin and the creek. They had yet to move into the old structure, which was badly in need of repairs before occupancy.

The day had been spent setting posts for a corral, riding herd of the horses. The animals were beginning to settle in well, what with water near and succulent graze wherever they strayed. Having eaten, the men leaned back against their saddles, smoking and talking about the work done and that needing to be done.

Al Rooney, sitting further away from the fire, turned his head, listening. Matt noticed his movement.

'Hear something, Al?' He knew the older cowboy was a range-wise individual. He had at least forty years behind him, perhaps more. He said little about his past, but from the way he handled weapons, worked horses and cattle, Matt realized Rooney was a tough nut and hard in certain ways. He'd once said, laconically, that out here a man was his own law and would be yet for some time to come. Matt knew this to be true. Law was coming and would be welcomed, but until then, the right of possession was a general rule and held true as long as you were capable of holding onto what you had attained.

Al nodded. 'Someone's comin'. Sounds like one hoss,' he answered in his soft, Texas drawl. Cold eyes looked at Matt. 'Best we get outta this here firelight, unless you're expectin' company.'

Matt shook his head.

'No one is coming that I know of. Move back into the shadows, boys.' His suggestion came too late.

A horseman rode up boldly, drawing his mount to a stop before Matt and the others could disappear into the shadows.

'Who's ramroddin' this outfit?' The face of the man was shadowed by the drooping brim of his hat.

Without glancing at Matt, Sam Tracy stepped out of the shadows and looked up at the rider.

'Who wants to know?'

The stranger, without speaking, dismounted and faced Sam, thereby breaking one of the courtesy codes of the West. He had not been invited to dismount. He straight-

24

ened and faced Sam and as he did so, Matt stepped up beside his friend.

'I'm the ramrod, as you call it. Why are you here?'

The stranger faced Matt. The hatbrim, pushed back, revealed, to Matt's surprise, the face of a young man. He can't be over twenty, if that, the thought ran through Matt's mind. Then he noticed that the sixgun on the man's right hip was swung low, and tied down with a thong. He's too young to be a shootist, Matt thought. A chill ran through him. This young man was an assassin, sent to make trouble or to kill.

'This basin belongs to Lear Holbrook, in Rimrock. He owns it free and clear–'

'You go back to Mr Holbrook, whoever he is, and tell him he is wrong. I own this basin. My papers are on file in the land office at Rimrock, and in the territorial capital of South Dakota. Now, you go on back and tell whoever sent you, that we are here legally and intend to stay.'

The young man laughed. 'You don't know who I am, do you? Well, you'll soon know my name is Thomas Lee Canfield, of the South Carolina Canfields. And my name will be up there right along with Wyatt Earp and Bill Thompson and others. Now, let's

25

get down to business.'

'And just what is that business?' asked Matt.

The man called Canfield squared away and faced Matt. 'I've come to kill you, whatever your name is. I'm calling you out!'

'Draw!'

CHAPTER THREE

'Did that kid, Canfield, or whatever his name is go out to the basin last night?'

Lear Holbrook lolled in his chair, lighting his first cigar of the day. He squinted his eyes through the smoke, looking at his companion, Lance Rainey. The gunman nodded.

'Yep. He'll be in here right soon to brag about his shootin', I expect.'

Holbrook grunted. 'We'll ride out there this morning and see about the rest of them.' He grinned at Rainey. 'A nice herd of horses for the army would bring in a pretty handful of cash money. We'll just take care of whoever is left of the owners, and cash in on what they have brought in.'

'Draw!'

The stranger's voice echoed against the backdrop of trees. His hand swept down to his sixgun and his fingers grasped the butt of the weapon.

Matt Curtis turned quickly sideways, and

27

raising his own pistol, fired as Canfield's weapon cleared leather. Canfield's bullet whistled past Matt's ear, a near miss, and his sixgun was eared back for a second shot when Matt's round struck him in the chest, boring through flesh and bone and tearing the heart apart.

Canfield stiffened and dropped his weapon, grasping his torn chest. His face was a mask of pain and surprise. He was a fast gun, as he had told everyone, and men had stepped aside for him. But here...? He staggered back and then fell, his boot-heels scrabbling momentarily at the loam. Then relaxed in death.

Matt relaxed. He shook his head and proceeded to eject the spent shell and reload the empty chamber of his sixgun. He holstered it, and shook his head again.

'I didn't want this,' he said softly, his face sad. 'He gave me no chance to talk with him. He was just ... a kid.'

'Kid or not,' said Tracy, 'he was loaded for bear, and out to get you.'

Matt looked down at the inert body for a long minute. He shook his head again.

'Wrap him up in his blanket, take care of his horse. In the morning we'll pay this Lear Holbrook a visit.'

Holbrook had just returned from breakfast at the hotel, when the swamper of the saloon knocked on his door. At Holbrook's 'It's open,' he opened the door and looked at his boss with a puzzled expression.

'There's a couple of rannys out in front and they told me to tell you to come out. They have something to give you.'

Holbrook stared at the man, the words slipping through his mind. Citizens of Rimrock did not order him to do anything, much less to leave his office at their bidding.

'Who are they? What do they want?' he grunted at the swamper. 'Are they regulars here?'

The swamper shook his head. 'Never saw them before in my life, boss. They just appeared and told me to tell you to come out there.'

Holbrook stirred himself and rose from his chair. This was not his usual response to such an order, for he was used to having men come to him, rather than himself going to them.

Scowling at the swamper he left the office and strode angrily through the saloon. At the batwing doors he slapped them apart and stepped out upon the porch. He glanced about and saw Matt and Al Rooney standing beside a blanket-wrapped object at his feet.

'What's this all about? Why are you bothering me? I'm a busy man.'

Matt stared at him coolly. Reaching down, he drew the blanket down from the head and shoulders of the dead Canfield. He straightened and looked at Holbrook.

The saloonkeeper was staring at the face of the dead man, a puzzled look on his face.

'What – who is this? I never saw this ranny before in my life.'

Lance Rainey appeared around the corner of the saloon and stepped up beside his boss. His eyes widened slightly at the sight of the dead man on the porch. He recognized the young gunman-to-be whom he had sent to the Basin. He shifted his gaze to Matt's face, then looked at Holbrook.

'This young man came into my camp last evening and called me out,' Matt told Holbrook. 'He told me he had come to kill me. And he gave me the name of the person who had hired him for the job.'

Holbrook's face was suddenly covered with sweat.

'What does that have to do with me? Or your dumping a body on my property?'

Matt eyed him grimly. Al Rooney moved to one side, so that he could see both Rainey and Holbrook. Rainey was armed with tied-down sixguns on both thighs. So far as Rooney could see, Holbrook was unarmed. Unless, of course, he had a hideaway in a pocket or up his sleeve, as gamblers and individuals of his type often had.

Matt was aware of Rooney's shifting positions, but he did not take his eyes from Holbrook's face. He was aware of the man's tenseness, seeing the paling of his face and the sweat on his cheeks.

'He gave Holbrook as the name of one who sent him.' Matt paused for a long moment, then spoke softly: 'I am told your name is Holbrook!'

Rainey's eyes narrowed and he lowered his hands to his gun butts.

'Hold it, right there!' Al Rooney's voice swept coolly across the space between him and Rainey. 'Keep your hands away from them pistols.'

Holbrook eyed Matt carefully, his anger and frustration cooling rapidly.

'Just who are you to take over at this point of the discussion? Mr Rainey is my *secundo*–'

'An' if there's gunplay, Mr Holbrook, or whoever you are, then you'll be the first to get it right in the belly, not your crony.'

Matt eyed Holbrook, his eyes cold and narrowed.

'I think you an' me had better have a conflab,' he said softly, 'before a war starts right here. What do you think?'

It was stalemate. Tension held tight reins. Holbrook glared at Matt and met the cool stare of determination. He suddenly realized that if Rainey made a move, he himself was a dead man. He sighed and waved Rainey away.

'Let it go, this time. Get rid of this body on my porch.' He eyed Matt carefully.

'You an' me are gonna have a talk. Come on in, we'll get to the bottom of this.'

CHAPTER FOUR

Emmy Henry stood on the porch of the hotel. She saw the tableau in front of the saloon and paled when she saw Holbrook's gunman entering the group. She was frightened by the man. He had made no moves toward her, but she knew he was behind much of the meanness going on in Rimrock. The regular marshal had left town and Holbrook had appointed one of his gang as the town marshal. Now the man strutted about giving orders and threatening mayhem to anyone who disagreed with him.

Now she saw Matt Curtis, and, apparently, one of his men arguing with Holbrook, and Rainey entering the confrontation. She shivered. She disliked Rainey, did not trust him, and had to force herself to be pleasant whenever he came in for meals.

She entered the building, went into the dining-room and began to lay the tables for the next meal. Her thoughts dwelt on the friendly young man she had met that one time. Matt Curtis had appealed to her and she hoped he would appear again for a meal. But that she had seen him talking with Lear Holbrook caused her unease. Anything pertaining to Holbrook or any of his cohorts, left her with an uneasy feeling.

Holbrook rounded his desk and flopped into his chair. He reached into the humidor, took a cigar from it and leaned back. Ignoring Matt Curtis, whom he had invited into his office, he proceeded to attend to his smoke.

Matt was aware of Holbrook's attitude. Holbrook was testing Matt's patience and calculating how far he could push the young rancher, if that was what he was. Aware of the reason behind the man's callousness, Matt relaxed and eyed the saloonkeeper quietly. He could wait as long as Holbrook, and his nerves were probably better than those of the saloonkeeper. Eventually, drawing smoke deeply into his lungs, then slowly exhaling it, Holbrook spoke.

'You are trespassing on my property,' he said evenly.

Matt eyed him.

'If you are referring to my being in the basin with my horses, you are wrong. I am not trespassing. I am on my own property.'

Holbrook's face flushed. He glared at

Matt and slapped a hand loudly on his desk.

'I have signed papers at the land office that shows I have rights to the basin. I give you two days to vacate, and if you ain't cleared out, you'll have to take the consequences!'

Matt put his hands on the edge of the desk. Leaning over, he looked directly into Holbrook's eyes.

'On my way here, I stopped at the territorial capital. I signed for ownership of the basin, based upon a letter giving me the inheritance of the property. If you have signed any papers saying you are the owner, then you are in the wrong. For the only signature was that of the person giving the basin to me. I'm in the basin to stay!'

'Get out of my office! You lie about signing anything, or having a letter giving you the rights. It is my land, and I give you two days to leave. Otherwise...'

Matt straightened. 'Don't bother to threaten me, Holbrook. It won't scare me. I'll be there when you are long gone from this area!' With that Matt turned and walked from the office.

Al Rooney was waiting him on the saloon veranda. Matt nodded toward the horses and the two mounted and rode out of the town.

'That Rainey feller was pinin' for a

showdown,' Rooney said. 'He looks like a gunslick, to me.'

'Holbrook ordered us out of the basin, Al. When we get back, we'll scatter the herd so they can't be rounded up, and get ready for any trouble he might send us.'

They came at full dark.

Horsemen rushed out of the night across the creek, sheltered by the dark shadows of the aspens. They attacked in a group, yelling and firing, riding across the camp-fire, scattering it, and shooting at the three men.

Matt rolled away from the firelight as the first hoof-sounds reached him, drawing his sixgun and firing at the looming form of a horseman bearing down upon him. His gun spat and the horseman swerved his mount, Matt's shot missing.

Sam Tracy had grabbed his rifle and, rolling to the edge of the firelight, was firing rapidly at the racing attackers. A man yelled in pain and the attackers swung their horses and raced back across the area, firing at the three men, cursing and yelling as they did so.

Matt lined up on one of the riders and fired rapidly.

The man swayed and, seizing the saddle horn, raced from the area, another racing after him. Suddenly they were gone. The basin became quiet. Horses disturbed by the sound of racing hoofs and blasts of gunfire, returned to grazing. Matt Curtis and Al Rooney looked at each other.

'That was sudden,' was Rooney's laconic comment. The fire was out, scattered by the hoofs of the horses racing through the camp. Matt remained where he was, reloading his sixgun, breathing heavily, his heart pounding in his chest. He eased himself up along the tree he had rolled behind during the fight.

'Sam, Al,' he called. 'Are you all right?'

Al's slow drawl drifted out of the shadows of the tree line.

'Hi, boss. Ain't hurt none. How about you?'

'I'm all right. Sam ... Sam?'

His partner did not answer. Realizing the attackers were gone, at least for the moment, Matt moved around the edge of the camp-site, looking into the darkness at the edge of the open space where they had pitched camp. A glint of metal caught his eyes.

Quickly he pushed some of the scattered fire-coals together and tossed some light wood and dried grass upon them. The material caught fire and blazed immediately. In the flickering light Matt saw his partner lying sprawled a few feet from the edge of the firelight.

'Sam!' Matt leaped to where his partner lay. He knelt and turned him on his back. Blank eyes stared up at him, glazing in the beginning rigors of death. A dark hole in the center of his forehead spoke of his instant death. His sixgun lay in his slack right hand.

His face twisted with emotion. Matt picked up the gun and spun the cylinder. All five rounds had been fired. As with most who worked cattle and horses, Sam left one empty chamber under the hammer for safety's sake.

Al came over and stood beside Matt, looking down at the young cowboy.

'Too young to die like that. Jist too young.' He shook his head and walked away. Matt sighed. He went to Sam's bedroll, brought a blanket and covered him.

'We'll dig his grave come light,' he told Al. 'The first grave in the basin, so far as I know.' He went to the fire and placed more fuel on it. 'Al, why don't you take a jaunt around and see if the horses are all right. I'll clean up around here.'

'Sure,' Al answered from the shadows. A few minutes later the sound of his horses hoofs came to Matt, splashing as he crossed the creek. Matt gathered up equipment scattered by the riders who had rushed through their campside. By the time Al returned, the camp was in order again and Matt had a pot of coffee going.

'The hosses has scattered some, skeered by the shootin', I reckon,' said Al. He poured himself a cup of the strong brew and settled back against his saddle. 'Cain't see as any are gone, at least not in the dark. Tell more come mornin'.'

Matt stared into the fire, the yellow flames reflecting on the flat, taut planes of his face. Al sat across from him, sipping his coffee, brooding.

'Y'all got any idea who done this?' Al asked, his cool eyes noting the sadness and questioning look on Matt's face.

Matt sighed and shook his head.

'None. I reckon, if you'll sorta watch the horses, after we bury Sam, I'll go into Rimrock and ask around some.'

Al shook his head.

'Not by yourself, you ain't. Boss, someone is out to get you. Whatever the reason, that wasn't no game they was playin' tonight. They meant business. They meant to kill everyone of us, an' right now I cain't put no reckonin' to it. But, if you're goin' into town, meanin' to ask questions an' draw a line on the ground, then I reckon I'll just mosey along an' keep watch on your back.'

CHAPTER FIVE

'We couldn't see just how many we hit,' the gunman said to Lear Holbrook. 'It was too dark. But I know I got one. I heard him yell and saw him fall.'

'How about this Curtis fellow? Did you take him out?' asked the saloonkeeper.

The man shook his head. 'Cain't say, boss. It was too dark and there was too much shootin' goin' on. I'll say this, it only took about two minutes, and in that time one of them in the dark, with a rifle, got three of our boys. One is a-layin' down at Ulysses Paine's place, gettin' dressed for a buryin'. And Hank and Bill are both at Doc's gettin' lead pulled out'n them. Someone out thar can really handle a rifle gun.'

Holbrook frowned. 'How about the horses? Did you see the horses enough to know how many there were and how good they looked?'

The man shook his head. 'I keep tellin' you, it was too dark, and we got out of there when that sharpshooter begin to drop our boys.'

Holbrook mused for a moment, his eyes looking beyond the man. His shadow, Lance Rainey, sat in his usual place, on a hard chair, to one side of the door. At last, Holbrook took a deep breath and spoke to the cowboy before him.

'Find Tip Wilson and send him in. Tell him I want him right now, not after he visits every bar and pats the fanny of every saloon girl in town.' Tip Wilson was foreman of Holbrook's LH ranch a few miles south of Rimrock.

The cowboy nodded and left. Holbrook looked at Rainey for a long moment.

'There were three of them. One was killed, maybe another wounded. Those horses are out there for the taking. A fine herd of animals, breeding stock, I suspect. We get them and sell them and who'll know how we came by them? You,' he stared hard at the gunman, 'you see to it that Curtis ain't around to bother us after it's done.'

When the foreman came in Holbrook had one order for him.

'Go in and take them horses out of Rimrock Basin an' put them in that high meadow on the north side of my range. Set a couple of men to see that they don't stray. I'll tell you when to move them again and to where.'

Wilson was a rangy man, grown silent and middle-aged on the plains and mountains of the West. He was paid a good salary by Holbrook to obey his boss. He simply nodded at the order and did not question it. Holbrook wanted the horses out of the basin and on his own meadows. That was all he needed to know. He touched his hatbrim to Holbrook, glanced at Rainey and left.

Back of the old cabin was a small knoll, topped by several tall pines and surrounded by aspen. Here Matt Curtis and Al Rooney cleared a space well back in the shade of the trees.

'Sam will be the first to be buried here,' Matt said. 'I aim to make this basin my home. There,' he pointed to the old cabin, 'I'll build my house and barns and sheds. This,' he looked about him, 'will be the family graveyard.' With no other words he chose a place and marked out the grave. Without speaking, Al joined him and together they dug the grave of their friend.

They wrapped Sam Tracy in his blankets and then folded his ground sheet about him. Matt cut a length of Sam's saddle lasso and wrapped the body tightly. Together they lowered it into the grave and refilled the

43

hole. They selected flat stones from the creek, hauled them to the site and covered the grave, to prevent animals from burrowing and disturbing the body.

Matt stepped back after the job was done. Al Rooney stood stoically to one side. Matt removed his hat and seeing the gesture Al uncovered his scant gray hair.

'Sam, old friend,' said Matt, a choking sensation in his throat, 'I ain't got no preacher to say the right words over you. But I guess the One upstairs understands my words just as well. You were a good friend, a man among men. You won't be forgotten.' After a long, quiet moment, he sighed and stepped back from the grave.

'Ah reckon no man could have better words spoken over him,' Al said softly.

The two men shouldered their shovels and walked back to the camp area. Matt immediately went to his horse and began saddling him. Al did the same. Matt made no mention that he had suggested the older man stay back and watch after the horses. His horse saddled, Matt mounted and glanced over at his companion. Rooney was already mounted and waiting. Both men were armed. Matt wore a Colt .45 on his right hip and carried a rifle in its sheath beneath his left leg.

Al Rooney was similarly armed, a Colt .44 on his left hip, butt forward, as for a cross-draw. He seldom wore the weapon. Matt had wondered about the unusual position of the sixgun, but had not mentioned it. A few gunmen of the West had used the cross-draw, but not many. To most it was awkward, demanding certain stance. Along with the sixgun Al also carried an old Winchester .44. The rifle and the sixgun both used the same ammunition.

Once in Rimrock, the two men hitched their horses to the rail before the saloon. Matt gestured toward the land office. 'I'm going there first.'

Al simply nodded.

'You go on,' he said. 'I'll look around awhile. Meet you back here in about a half-hour?' Matt nodded and the two parted.

When Matt opened the land office door, Howie Burkhart looked up from a paper he was reading and nodded.

'I thought you'd be showin' up afore long,' he said. 'I heard there had been a raid on your camp.'

Matt leaned on the counter and looked with cold eyes into the land agent's face.

'Burkhart, has there been anyone filed on

the basin before me?'

Howie laid down the paper he was reading and frankly returned Matt's stare. He shook his head.

'Nope. And the papers you brought in makes you the owner, providing you are able to hold onto it.'

'Then someone don't like my being there,' Matt said. His eyes never left those of the land agent. 'Do you have any idea who is interested enough to kill for the basin?'

Al Rooney followed Matt into the Rimrock saloon. He moved quietly aside as he stepped through the batwing door, his keen gaze moving quickly about the room. It was near noon. There were some business owners taking their midday drink, talking with each other seated at tables about the large room. Three cowboys leaned on the bar sipping their drinks and talking quietly.

Matt moved up to the bar and gestured for the bartender.

'Where is Holbrook's office?'

At his question talk ceased and the room became silent. The three cowboys at the bar turned and eyed him, taking in the broad shoulders and deep chest of the young man, and the fact that the slim rider's sixgun was slung on his right hip.

Most of all they caught the glint of anger in the gray-green eyes, slashing across the room at them. The bartender moved down the length of the pine bar toward him.

'Who wants to know?'

Matt eyed him and then the three cowboys who had turned to survey him. One of them looked at the barkeep and shook his head.

'Is that his office?' Matt nodded toward the door at the end of the bar, which stood slightly ajar.

'I wouldn't know, stranger,' said the barkeep. 'If you want a drink I'll serve you. If you want some grub, there's some beef sandwiches or crackers or cheese for you along with your drink. I'm not a signpost givin' out directions or information to every shirt-tail cowpoke that comes along.'

Matt nodded curtly. 'Very well. Then you'll just go on about your business, while I go see what's behind that door there.' He moved down the room, which had remained completely silent. Those at the tables in the room watched without comment. The three cowboys drew slightly apart as Matt moved.

'Now, you boys jist stay right where you are.' A quiet voice reached across the room to them. They looked toward the saloon entrance. Al Rooney stood slightly away from the wall, his eyes on the cowboys. 'Jist turn back to the bar an' continue your drinkin',' he told them.

The stance of the man, the cold gleam of his eye, his right hand thumb-hooked lightly above his belt buckle, close to the black, well-worn butt of his sixgun, worn cross-draw on his left hip, were not lost upon the cowboys.

Matt opened the door and stood looking for Lear Holbrook, who reared back in his chair and glared at the intruder. Lance Rainey came to his feet, his deep-set eyes boring into Matt's face. His slim hand, covered as usual by a thin leather glove, hovered above his right hand sixgun.

Matt nodded toward Rainey, but spoke directly to Holbrook, his eyes never leaving the bar-owner's face.

'Tell your guard dog there to sit down and be very, very still. It won't be him my bullet finds, if he draws that six. It'll be you.'

Holbrook eased back in his chair, his eyes on Matt's right hand, near the black butt of his sixgun. He knew by the tone of voice and the narrowing of his eyes that this man meant exactly what he said. He gestured to Rainey.

'Sit. Be quiet.'

The lanky gunman stared for a moment longer at the intruder and then did as his boss ordered. His eyes never left Matt's face, and his hand remained near the sixgun on his right hip.

'Who are you? What do you mean by bustin' in here like a bull in a china shop?' asked Holbrook bluntly.

'My name is Curtis, Matt Curtis. Some of your men slammed through my camp last night and gunned down one of my men.'

'Now, that is quite an accusation,' Holbrook growled. He reached into the humidor on his desk and removed a long, black cigar. 'What kind of proof do you have to back up such talk?' He took a match from his vest pocket and lit the cigar.

'I was just over to Doc Marcus's office. He had one of your men there. The man will live; I shot him when he attacked my camp. The doc told me he was one of your boys. Now, that seems proof enough for me.'

Holbrook puffed on the cigar and blew a plume of smoke toward Matt.

'The basin is mine. You run some horses in there where I mean to bring a herd. Get out of the basin and there will be no trouble. Better yet, just get out of the area. We don't need no horse ranch here, if that is what you have in mind starting.'

Matt shook his head. 'Nope. You haven't filed on the basin. I was just up to the land office. I have filed'

Holbrook straightened. 'No one has filed on that land yet. I looked at the books yesterday.'

'Then how about this?' Matt took an envelope from his pocket, removed a single sheet of paper and tossed it onto the desk in front of the saloon owner.

Holbrook looked at him briefly, and then picked up the paper and read it. His eyes narrowed and his face reddened. The paper shook in his hands. He read it again and then deliberately folded it and handed it back to Matt.

'Anyone can have anybody write a letter like that. So it says you inherited it from someone named Clarence Bowman. That don't mean a thing.'

Matt smiled coldly. 'It does when it is on record at the State Capital Land Office,' he said. 'The basin is mine, Holbrook. You had your men jump me last night thinking to scare me away. My partner was killed. I can't prove who fired the shot that killed him, but you engineered the raid. I'm holding you responsible and intend going to

50

the sheriff about it. In the meantime, the basin is mine. Stay out of it!'

Holbrook eyed Matt silently, his face stoic, but his eyes gleamed with anger and hate. Suddenly he exploded.

'Take him, Lance!' he yelled, slamming his chair back against the wall. 'Now!' His hand darted to the desk and yanked at a drawer.

Lance Rainey leaped to his feet, his right hand darting to his gun belt.

Matt seized the heavy wooden humidor and flung it at Rainey. Then, crouching, he grabbed for his sixgun, knowing that he was no match for the gunman in the corner of the room. His attention instead was on Holbrook, apparently scrambling to get a weapon from a drawer in the desk.

'Everyone hold it! Right now!' Al Rooney's voice lashed through the noise of the room. He stood in the doorway, his gun trained on Holbrook.

Matt backed away from the line of fire and Rainey paused with his sixgun half-drawn, his eyes taking in the blue steel gleam of the weapon that was held unwaveringly in the tanned fist of its owner.

'Rooney?' Lance Rainey whispered, a hiss that spoke of frustration and anger. 'Al Rooney?'

'The same,' Rooney said quietly. 'Just let your gun slide back in the leather an' set down in your chair with your hands where I kin see 'em.' He wriggled the gunbarrel at Holbrook. 'You set down, too!'

His face purple with fury, the saloon owner did as he was ordered, his hands on the desk before him. Rainey eased down into his chair, his eyes burning on the face of the man in the doorway, his face expressionless.

'Have you palavered all you want with these rannies?' Al asked Matt, without taking his eyes from the two men.

'I reckon. Our next move is to talk with the sheriff. I want him to know all about it, and let him do a little talkin' with Holbrook and his lapdog here.'

Rainey tensed at being called a lapdog, but he eased as the bore of Al's sixgun shifted over to bear upon him.

Holbrook relaxed a little.

'Why, Mr Curtis, that's your name, ain't it? You go right ahead and talk with the sheriff. You'll find that I was in my rights about the basin. It's mine and you have no rights there, regardless of what this letter says.'

Matt picked up the letter from the desk

52

and stepped into the barroom, his eyes quickly sweeping the interior. Sensing trouble, the men who'd been at the tables had left the saloon. The barkeep stood halfway down the bar, polishing a glass, his ears tuned to the voices coming from the office. When Matt appeared, he turned away and began working on the bar itself.

Al Rooney stepped out of the office door and pulled it shut behind him. The two left the bar side by side, glancing warily right and left as they stepped out upon the boardwalk.

'Al, you go on back to the basin and watch the horses,' Matt said. 'I am going to walk around town and ask a few questions. I should be back by dark.'

Al nodded stoically. 'Watch your back,' he murmured. He stepped off the boardwalk and mounted his horse. In a few minutes he disappeared beyond the stand of aspen that bordered the trail entrance to the town.

Matt found himself walking toward the hotel. He recalled the sweet face of Emmy Henry and the good meal she had set before him. Another plate of beef and spuds might go good, he thought, with those strong, young hands serving it.

When he entered the dining-room he saw

53

that Emmy was not present. A heavyset woman came from the kitchen and looked at him.

'D'ya want to eat? I ain't got much goin',' she said.

'Maybe later,' he told her. 'Is Emmy around?'

'She's most likely up in their rooms,' the woman said, pointing upward. 'Her pa's hurt real bad and she's takin' care of him fer a few days until he's on his feet again. Go on up; she'll probably be glad fer a little company. Last door on the right off the hall.'

Matt thanked her and climbed the stairs. At the end of the hall he knocked softly on the last door. Footsteps approached from within and the door opened. Emmy stood facing him. Her face lighted up with a smile when she saw who stood there. She stepped back and opened the door wider.

'Come in, Matt,' she invited. He entered and she closed the door behind him. He noticed dark circles under her eyes and her hand trembled. She had glanced hurriedly down the hallway before she closed the door.

'Is something wrong?' he asked, as she turned to him again. Tears came to her eyes.

'My father,' she said with trembling voice. 'Someone beat him nearly to death two days ago. The doctor is not sure he will live.'

Impulsively, he reached out and put his arms about her, drawing her close to him. Her arms went about his waist and she pressed her face to his chest, and sobbed.

Holding her, feeling her pain and her need to weep, he thought of the future and wondered, briefly, how and if Emmy Henry would be there.

CHAPTER SIX

Al Rooney arrived back at the basin slightly before dark. Going to the usual campsite in front of the old cabin, he cared for his horse and busied himself making camp. It was full dark and he did not attempt to check on the horse herd. An hour or so after a supper of beef stew that he had made, with some hard, saved-over biscuits, he moved several yards from the fire and, rolled in his blankets, settled in for the night.

Rooney was up at first light and, after a breakfast of coffee, biscuits and a slice of broiled beef, he saddled his horse and set out to make a count of the horses that he, Sam and Matt had brought into the basin.

He came to the meadows where they had allowed the horses to spread and graze. Easing in the saddle, he swept a long look over the area. Indications of grazing and rolling in the grasses were there, but there were no horses. He rode the rolling meadows, filled with deep, lush grazing. Here and there he saw a stray that had escaped whoever had made a hurried gather of the animals. For that was what had happened, Al Rooney realized. Someone had come into the basin and driven out the horses he and Matt and Sam had spent so long gathering and developing – the seed, the core of their planned ranch for finely bred mounts.

There was a demand for such horses; the army was always a ready market, as were the larger ranches. Cattle ranchers had no time to breed and raise and train horses needed for range work. They were bought from those who had bred and trained the animals for them. This had been the plan, to be the breeders, the trainers and the source of excellent mounts for this part of Wyoming.

Now someone had stolen their herd and with the herd went the basis of their future horse ranch.

Al Rooney was a methodical man. He and Matt had visited the basin after Clarence Bowman, Matt's uncle, his mother's brother, had willed it to Matt. Bowman had died without immediate heirs, and for years had lived with the Curtises in southern Idaho.

Upon his death, the basin had been singled out in his will as being bequeathed to Matt. Bowman had filed on the land many years previously on account of a deposit he and a miner friend had located on one side of the basin. It was all explained in a single sheet attached to the will. The letter explained briefly that Bowman considered the basin worth far more as a ranch for some special breeding actively, than for any minerals beneath the surface. Al Rooney knew all this.

What he had to do right now, was to search until he found where the horses had left the basin, and follow those tracks until he located the herd.

Grimly, carefully, he searched the entire basin, taking two entire days to cover the 60,000 acres, standing on high points and looking over miles below him. Lush grazing, cool streams and shady stands of pine, piñon and aspen were before him. Only a few stray that had escaped from the herd appeared here and there.

At last, at the end of the third day, as darkness was closing in, he found a trail. A herd of 200 horses cannot move quickly from one point to another without leaving sign. This he knew and was depending upon. Once found, he followed until darkness closed in and it was impossible to see the tracks.

He made a cold camp, eating jerky and drinking water from a clear, flowing stream. He lighted no fire and did not smoke. He took no chance of being seen or heard by those who had run off with the herd. Wrapped in his blankets, with his sixgun at hand and the rifle within quick reach, he slept lightly, knowing that if something or someone came within sight or sound, his horse would alert him.

He was up and in the saddle at first light. The trail was strong. Apparently no caution had been taken while driving the herd from the basin. It was high noon before he realized the herd had not actually been driven from the basin. He found them in a small canyon, leading off into the higher slopes of the Laramie Mountains.

The mouth of the canyon was narrow. Those who had driven the herd into the canyon had hurriedly closed off the entrance by felling a pine across it, and piling brush and debris from deadfalls upon it. The barrier was neither stable nor permanent, but it would suffice for a short time to keep the animals in place.

Rooney tied his horse in the midst of a thick copse of aspen and worked his way silently through the barrier and into the canyon. In a few minutes he found the guard. One man leaned lazily against a boulder, smoking, half-asleep. Beyond him the canyon widened and Rooney could see a camp with two other men moving about. Beyond them were the horses, spread out over a small, lushly grassed meadow. However, with that many horses, and the meadow being small, what graze there was would soon be gone. This meant the herd had to be moved very soon.

As silently as he had come, Al Rooney moved out of the canyon. He knew where the horses were. The information had to be got to Matt. He untied his horse and thrust a foot into the stirrup.

Something slammed against the side of his head from behind and he fell, dazed, unable to move. Another blow rendered him unconscious. The morning light spiraled down into darkness. He lay sprawled and bleeding at the feet of Tip Wilson, the foreman of the LH spread.

Wilson nudged Rooney with a foot. There was no response. He nodded and grinned. 'We'll just tie this feller up an' keep him 'til we see what the boss wants done with 'im, he thought to himself. He stooped, lifted Rooney, and threw him roughly over his saddle. He mounted behind Rooney and, balancing the body with one hand, Wilson guided the horse back into the canyon and into the camp.

'Caught me a spy,' he announced to the other three men grouped about the fire. 'Reckon he's with that Curtis feller that brung them hosses in. We'll just keep him here 'til I kin find out what the boss wants done with 'im.'

Matt Curtis winced as he leaned over and looked into the bruised and battered face of Silas Henry. Emmy stood beside him, her eyes tearful and tired.

'Who did this?' Matt asked. He noticed that the chest of the elderly man was tightly bound, indicating broken ribs, if not more.

Emmy shook her head. 'We don't know. Daddy hasn't spoken since the man who worked around the stables found him and brought him home. I ran and got Doctor Marcus immediately and he has done all he can for Daddy. He said that at his age, he might not...' Her voice choked and she turned away, her hands over her face.

Matt turned and patted her shoulder, his face showing his sympathy.

'Doctors are sometimes wrong, Emmy.

And your pa is made of the stuff of pioneers who brought this country this far. I've got a feeling he'll make it.'

Suddenly she turned and leaned against his chest, burying her face against him. She burst into tears, sobbing, and Matt took her in his arms. He brushed her long, soft hair with his hand, pressing her to him.

She shuddered in her grief and her arms went about his shoulders, her soft womanliness pressed firmly against his body. A feeling ran through him, causing his heart to pound and his mind to whirl. He had known women, but not Emmy's kind. Her sweetness, her innocence and her grief all touched him to the core and suddenly he knew this was the woman he wanted with him for the rest of his life. His arms pressed her close, her soft breath touching his neck. Lowering his head, he kissed her cheek and rocked her gently in his arms.

At last she sighed and drew away slowly. Her face suddenly flamed and her hands went to her lips, her eyes wide and staring into him.

'I ... I... Please don't think...' she stammered.

He shook his head. 'I think you are a very sad girl, needing someone to hold onto for awhile, and I was here. That's what I think. Later we might talk more.'

She continued looking into his face, then lowered her eyes, a soft smile trembling upon her lips.

He shook himself slightly. He led her from the room and seated her at a small table on which rested a picture, apparently of her as a young girl. It was a charcoal-and-chalk sketch, as made by a traveling artist. A Bible was also on the table, under the shade of an oil-lamp, placed upon a clean, white doily.

He seated himself in a straight chair across from her.

'Emmy, was your dad the only one beaten up like this?'

She shook her head. 'No. Tom Clogg, who owns the general mercantile, was beaten badly also,' she told him. 'In fact, the doctor says he is hurt somewhere inside.'

'If no one knows who beat them like this, does anyone know *why* they were beaten up?' he asked.

She reached over and touched his hand. A frightened look came into her eyes. 'I know why, but it is dangerous to even talk about it.'

'I won't mention where my information came from,' he said, squeezing her hand.

She let her hand rest in his, as a small bird would snuggle into a nest. He could feel her pulse, her heart was racing.

After a moment, she answered: 'All right. I will tell you what *probably* caused it. Lear Holbrook came into Rimrock and set up his own law, run out the sheriff – had him killed, my father thinks – and appointed his own sheriff. He told the town council that it was to keep outlaws and hoodlums from cheating the people and from rousing the town every time they came in.'

She paused and drew a long, shuddering breath, then continued: 'For this service, each businessman, and each family head must pay a protection fee. It would pay the salaries of the marshal and the sheriff, and cover other contingencies, whatever that means. The fee has been raised twice and at the time that Dad and Mr Clogg were beaten, it was to be raised again. Ten more dollars a month from every businessman, the head of every household. Dad hasn't been able to say, but Mrs Clogg told me that Tom said he and Dad refused to pay any more protection fees. That was why they were both beaten so badly.'

Matt nodded grimly. 'They were made object lessons for the rest of the community.

What about the town itself? Isn't there a town council, or a mayor who can do something about this gang of thieves?'

'They all thought at first that it was a good idea,' she said, 'to have someone take over and clean out the outlaw element. Of course, we know now it was the pot calling the kettle black! They were willing to pay for the protection. But, now, they are all frightened to death of Lear Holbrook and that gunman of his, Lance Rainey.'

'Rainey looks like a real bad *hombre,*' Matt said. 'But Holbrook, well he seems like a snake in the grass, all right. But I suspect that without his gunman by his side, he doesn't look nearly so dangerous.'

'Looks are deceiving, Matt, in his case. He is a mean man, and used other bad men to do his bidding. He is in control of Rimrock and most of the territory now, and intends to keep a hold on it.'

Matt patted her hand and rose. 'Well, maybe someone needs to change his mind slightly.' He smiled at her. 'I think just maybe that can be done.'

She stood and followed him to the door.

He eyed her seriously. 'I hope your dad gets better soon. He's a strong man. I think he'll be all right. Just keep him away from the livery for a day or two.' He looked at her for a few moments more, then bent and kissed her lips gently. He turned and left the room, closing the door quietly behind him.

He also left Emmy with a blushing face and trembling lips. Her mind was awhirl. There had been suitors since the period of life when her womanhood had ripened and become evident. She had gone to community dances and on picnics with various young men of the town, or with cowboys off the nearby ranches. There had been times when her heart pounded over a brief kiss or a touch of a hand on her body. But this was different. Her world seemed to sing and her heart thrilled! Never had she felt like this when she had been kissed by a date.

She sighed and turned back to the bedroom where her father had suddenly groaned. Then, for the first time since he had been brought to her, he called for her in a weak voice.

It was mid-afternoon. Matt brought his horse from in front of the saloon where he had left it, and walked it to the livery barn. There he pumped water into a trough in front of the stables and stood as the horse drank deep draughts from the cool water.

'Your name is Curtis?'

Matt turned and saw three men lolling in the large open door of the livery. They looked like the usual town troublemakers, except for one. He was big, well over six feet tall and heavy with it. His face showed the effects of having been battered in many brawls, and there were only two fingers on his left hand. All three were armed, sixguns slung low upon their right hips. They were not dressed as any cowpuncher off the range, with chaps and spurred boots, but in the jackets and trousers of townsmen.

'Yeah. I'm Curtis. Who wants to know?'

Suddenly a gun appeared in the hand of one of the men.

'Just step into the livery,' the big fellow said. 'We want to talk to you about something.'

Matt raised his hands. He immediately suspected he was to be the victim of a beating, engineered by Lear Holbrook. A rude invitation to leave town. He walked into the barn, warily watching the three men, the one with the gun walking behind him, the other two on either side. They crowded him into a large stall and the big man with the crippled hand shut the gate behind them.

The one holding the gun holstered it quickly and in the same movement slammed a blow at Matt's chin. Expecting some such move, Matt ducked and kicked out at the one nearest, landing a blow to the man's belly. The fellow yelled in pain and fell back against the side of the stall.

Whirling, Matt saw the big, two-fingered man coming at him. Matt held to the belief that a quick offense was the best defense and launched a vicious blow to the man's midsection. The big fellow belched, but moved back only scant inches. His huge, hamlike fist connected with the side of Matt's head and Matt saw more stars than ever before in his life. He fell back dazed, and the three attackers took advantage of the moment. All were at him at the same time, hemming him in, slugging him with knotted fists.

Matt knew he was going to get the beating of his life. However, he did not realize the men were after his life. Not until one of them seized a sixgun and began slashing at his head with it. The steel connected with his skull and Matt groaned and fell, sprawling, in the dirt and straw of the stall.

The one who hit him cocked his sixgun and leveled it at Matt's inert form.

'Hey,' said one, 'you gonna shoot him? Right here in broad daylight?'

'Rainey said Holbrook wanted him done away with,' the one holding the gun said.

'Yeah ... but ... wait, someone's comin'.'

Quickly the sixgun was shoved into leather and the three men scurried out of the stall and ran from the barn through a back door.

Old Eli Strump was the town drunk. Once a businessman in the East, he had lost everything in a fire, including a wife and child. Devastated with grief, he simply walked away from his life and into the bottle. He wandered West and finally ended up in Rimrock, a roustabout in the saloons, working for a dollar now and then, just enough for a meal and a night lost in hours of dazed drunkenness. He slept in one of the livery stalls and helped Silas Henry with the work in return for the favor. With Silas unable to care for the livery, he had sobered enough to take over the work until the owner returned.

Shaking with the need to drown himself in a bottle, he slouched into the barn and heard a groan coming from of the stalls. He found Matt lying in a pool of blood and muttered to himself:

Better get the doc... This feller looks bad off.

CHAPTER SEVEN

Al Rooney could see all that went on around the camp-fire. It was past supper and the men were smoking and talking. One of them passed around a bottle of rotgut whiskey taken from his saddlebags.

'You sure know what kind of food to bring along,' one of the men said with a smirk.

'Nothin' like livin' high on the hog,' the owner of the bottle replied.

Al had continued to test his bonds ever since he had been tossed off his horse beside the camp. They had been checked once since his arrival, by one called 'Slag', whom he surmised was the one in charge of the stealing of the herd.

His bonds were tight, but not painful. Rooney had slender hands and wrists. He twisted and turned them slowly, making certain he made no quick movements which would attract the attention of the three men. From their talk he had learned that the foreman of the LH ranch would be out sometime the next day to decide where the horse herd would be taken. Since Matt Curtis had claimed possession of the basin, the animals could not be kept there.

Al Rooney lay beneath a small clump of pine. His saddle and blankets had been stripped from his horse, and the animal hazed in with the herd. His rifle had been taken, along with his sixgun, and tossed beside one of the men's bedrolls. Al could see them from where he lay.

The bonds were slowly loosening. He pulled and twisted until slowly one hand came free, then the other. He lay with his hands behind his back, watching the men about the camp-fire. In his right boot was a slim, keen knife. Once the men at the fire rolled into their blankets, he would be able to free himself completely.

It was not long before the horses were checked once more. Slag walked over and looked down at Rooney.

'Guess you'll be all right 'til mornin',' he said. 'You just keep quiet an' we'll see what the boss man wants done with you.' Al did not answer him. Slag turned and sauntered back to the fire.

'Jack,' he called to one of the men. 'You kinda keep watch 'til midnight. Then Olly will spell you 'til three or four, and I'll take over then.'

Jack grunted and settled himself against his saddle, with his rifle leaning on his bedroll at hand.

'That Rooney feller settled in for the night?' he asked Slag.

'Yeah, he's all right. He won't give us any trouble.'

Rooney watched the three men who'd been sitting around the fire, his eyes closed to slits to suggest he was sleeping. The two men, Slag and Olly, were already quiet in the blankets, their hats over their eyes. Jack, on watch, leaned against his saddle, looking into the dying camp-fire. He glanced across at Rooney once or twice, and seeing the captive quiet and seemingly asleep, he twisted into a more comfortable position and sat dreaming, looking into the camp-fire.

It was not long before Rooney saw the guard's head drop in a nod. Jack jerked awake and looked hurriedly over at his companions and then at their captive. Seeing his companions asleep and Rooney quiet, his head lowered, his hat shadowing his face. The guard sat staring, bored and tired, into the fire. In a few minutes his head nodded again. He jerked awake and glanced about, twisted in his position and settled again. In a few minutes his head nodded once more and remained lowered. A low snore came up the slope to where Al Rooney lay.

Rooney remained quiet until he was certain the guard was soundly asleep. His hands were free. Cautiously he slipped the knife from his boot top and freed his feet. He rose silently and stood looking at his captors. His face hardened his pale eyes narrowed mercilessly. Moving slowly and noiselessly, he crept to where his rifle and sixgun lay, as they had been tossed when he had been roughly dumped from his horse, after being slammed on the back of the head by Slag's rifle butt. He quietly fastened the belt with his sixgun about his middle and took up the rifle.

He walked quietly over to the sleeping guard and, without ceremony, slammed his own rifle butt to the man's head. With a loud grunt, the man crumbled against his saddle.

Awakened by the grunt, Slag turned in his blanket, tossed his hat from covering his eyes, and stared into the black, menacing bore of Al's rifle.

'You jist get up real quiet-like,' Rooney said in a soft, steely voice. 'Take your lariat an' tie up your partner yonder.' He gestured to Olly, who was stirring at the sound of voices.

'What in ... how'd...' Slag stared at the

slack body of the guard.

'Never mind. Jist do as I say, or I'll put a hole through your gut an' let you lay there and die. Which you actually deserve.'

Slag scrambled to his feet. He jerked his lariat from his saddle horn, then stepped over and slammed a toe into Olly's side.

'Hey ... what'd you do that for? Dang it, Slag, one of these days–'

'Shut up an' stand up!' Slag reached down and jerked his partner to his feet. He turned him around and began binding his hands behind him.

Rooney stepped around in front of him and thrust the rifle against his nose.

'Now, you make up your mind, buster. Either get tied up or take a bullet through your nose. An' it make no difference to me which I do!'

Olly hurriedly thrust his arms behind him. Slag tied his wrists and lower arms. While this was happening, the guard shook his head and raised it. Immediately he saw what was happening. Rooney did not see him as he snaked his sixgun from his holster and trained it upon him. But the click of the hammer being cocked sounded like a drum roll in the midnight silence.

Rooney shoved Olly into Slag. As the two

75

fell, he dived to the ground and rolled over. The guard's slug whined over his head. It was the only round the guard released. Rooney's rifle spat and spat again. A small blue hole appeared in the guard's forehead and his heart was burst by the second bullet which slammed into his side. He fell back and shuddered and died.

Slag leaped to his feet and lunged for the rifle near his bedroll. Rooney's third bullet exploded the dust in front of his feet and he skidded to a halt. Olly lay where he was, struggling with his bonds.

'Pick up your pal there, an' drag him up that slope,' Al ordered the sullen Slag. 'I'll bring the other one.'

Slag seized the guard's legs and did as Rooney ordered. Olly scrambled awkwardly to his feet and followed them, with Rooney directly back of him, alertly watching every move.

In a few minutes Rooney had both Olly and Slag bound to a pine, with their partner lying dead at their feet. Without glancing at his captives, he returned to the camp-fire. He got their weapons and flung them as far into the darkness of the trees and bushes as possible.

'Hey, there,' Slag yelled from where he was bound with Olly to the pine tree. 'We'll never find our irons flung into the woods that way. That ain't human.'

Still silent, Rooney walked away from the camp and whistled softly. He called again. There was a scuff of hoofs and his horse appeared out of the night, snuffling at the familiar scent of his long-time master. Rooney led the horse to the camp and saddled it, using tack belonging to one of his captives.

Trailing the reins, he then approached the men bound to the tree.

'I put you up here out of the way. I'm gonna run that herd of our hosses right through here. You might get bumped, even where you are, but I'd reckon you're out of the way. I heard you say your foreman was comin' tomorrow. You tell him the hosses is scattered to hell an' gone. An' I'm gonna be ridin' this basin night an' day. Th' first ranny I see tryin' to steal our hosses agin, will get a rifle bullet wherever I kin put it. I'll be out there, an' you won't know when it's gonna happen. Now, you tell him so he understands, hear?'

With that, Al Rooney gigged his horse and rode back into the small canyon. Daybreak was painting the skyline in pinks and rose. By the time he had the horses stirring and moving toward the mouth of the canyon, it would be almost full light. A stampede

77

would break the flimsy barrier the three men had dragged across the canyon and he could then take the rest of the day to haze the herd to the far side of the basin and spread it, making it impossible for the horses to be gathered again for several days.

Grimly he set to work, his horse darting and cutting, rounding up the horses, until finally he had them grouped between the narrow walls of the canyon. Behind them he raised his sixgun and fired into the air, the roar of the shot reverberating loudly from the canyon walls. The lead mare of the herd leaped and ran, others following her, until the entire herd was racing toward the narrowed mouth of the canyon. The flimsy barrier of brush and small trees across the opening of the canyon was no impediment to the rushing herd and in a five minutes time, it was free of the defile and spreading out across the basin.

Al Rooney raced behind the lead mare and hazed her away from the canyon and toward the far rim of the basin. In a few minutes all the two bound members of the Holbrook gang could hear was the sound of the wind in the pines, and the gurgle and splash of a small creek running through the center of the canyon.

CHAPTER EIGHT

The face was hazy against the white background of the ceiling. Matt squinted and his vision cleared. She smiled and adjusted the cover about his chest.

'You are finally awake.' Emmy Henry touched his hand and then sat on the edge of the bed.

'Where am I? What happened?' Matt was dizzy and he shut his eyes for a moment.

'You are in my bedroom, across the hall from Dad.' Emmy Henry told him. 'Someone attacked you in the livery stable and after Doctor Marcus examined you, I had them bring you here. You will have to tell us what happened; we don't know who did this to you.'

Matt attempted to move and a sharp pain in his side made him gasp.

'Someone did a pretty good job on me,' he muttered. 'My ribs feel stove in and my head aches like a mesa fell on it.'

'You have a bad gash on your head and there are two ribs cracked. The doctor said the head will heal quickly, but you will have to take it easy for about a month before you can do any riding or any more fighting.' A faint smile came to her lips.

'Well, it looks like I came out all right,' he said wryly, his lips twisting into a smile. 'But how come I am here in your place? You have enough to do, taking care of your pa.'

She shrugged. 'Old Eli Strump found you in the livery and ran and got the doctor. The doctor had you taken to his office and fixed you up the best he could. The news came to the hotel and I went to Doc's office to see just how badly you were hurt. One thing led to another and I offered to keep and care for you. After all, I already had one cripple. Another wouldn't be much more work.'

'And I do thank you,' he said, reaching out and touching her hand. 'How long have I been here?'

She thought a moment. 'This is the morning of the second day. You woke up last evening, but the doctor was here and gave you another dose of laudanum so you'd sleep well for at least one more night. I'll bet you're starved.'

'I am hungry,' he admitted. 'Has Al Rooney been around? He's my foreman and partner in horse ranching.'

80

'Who?' She had risen and was going to the door.

'Al Rooney. He's working the horse herd with me. Little shorter than me, getting gray over the ears, a quiet-like man.'

She shook her head. 'No. No one like that has come around.' Her hand was on the doorknob. 'By the way, I have some bean soup and cornbread in the kitchen and coffee going. Would you like some?'

He nodded. 'That sounds like a feast to me.' He turned his thoughts to the horse herd and the fact that Al Rooney had not been about for over two days.

Matt Curtis healed fast. The day following his return to full consciousness, he insisted in rising and dressing. Reluctantly, Emmy gave him his clothes, newly washed and ironed and ready to wear. His ribs were cracked on the left side and were bound tightly. He winced at a stab of pain as he twisted to adjust his pants. By the time Emmy returned to the room, he was standing at the window looking out onto the main street.

'How did it go?' she asked.

He turned to her with a wry smile.

'A little reminder here and there that someone wanted me put away for good. But thanks to the doctor, and to you, they'll be disappointed. I think I'll live!'

She laughed. 'If we can keep you still long enough,' she said.

'Why does the town allow Holbrook to run roughshod over everything?'

She shrugged. 'He has his own sheriff and his own town marshal. I suspect the judge is in his pocket, also. He is the law. If he says give, they have to give, or they'll end up as Pa and you and Mr Clogg, the storekeeper.'

'Everyone is afraid of him … them?'

She nodded. 'A few others have tried to have the town council remove the marshal and hire one of their own. But the council is afraid to act. It's true, the bad element that used to bother us, break up a saloon, or race up and down Front Street and shoot at anything that moved, is pretty well cleaned out. But it's beginning to look like the cure is as bad or worse than the disease,' she concluded.

Al Rooney showed up the day after Matt got out of bed and dressed. He found his boss sitting on the front porch of the hotel, reading a month-old newspaper.

Rooney wrapped the reins of his horse about the rail in front of the hotel, came up the two steps and squatted against the veranda post nearest Matt. Matt grinned at him wryly.

'I found me a bump on the noggin after you left. What's goin' on in the basin?'

Rooney raised an eyebrow. 'Kinda rough people in this town, huh? Waal, there's some so-called rough people after our hosses, too.'

Matt looked at him intently. 'What happened?' he asked.

Rooney related his capture, escape and the spreading of the herd in the far reaches of the basin.

'You shot one of them?'

Rooney nodded. 'Yep. Holbrook's foreman was supposed to show up yesterday and tell his men what to do with our hosses. I suspect Holbrook knows about the shootin' by now.'

'Then we'll be hearing from them pretty soon, I suspect,' said Matt. 'Very well.' He thought for a moment and then looked at Rooney. 'Come on in and Emmy'll fix you a meal you won't forget. We'll talk about what can be done while you eat.'

Over the meal of steak and eggs, mugs of coffee and half an apple pie, Rooney brought Matt up to date on the happenings in the basin. Matt did the same concerning his beating and what he had found out about the town being under the thumb of Lear Holbrook and his cohorts.

As they sat sipping their coffee, eased back in the chairs, Matt mused for several minutes. They were far enough away from other customers in the restaurant to be able to converse freely in low voices and not be overheard. Several glances probed them and Matt was certain some of those looking them over were in the pay of Holbrook.

'Al.' Matt finally stirred and spoke. 'See if you can find two or three men here in town who are looking for work. Take 'em to the basin an' round up the horses. Find a place where the horses can be held easily without building another complete corral, an' hold 'em there. One of you be on guard all the time. If Holbrook's men try to run you out an' get horses, hold 'em off the best you can. But don't get yourselves killed. If you see you can't beat them, then let the horses go. Remember that there's a brand on each of the horses where few people would think to look. We can find them later.'

'What are you gonna do here in town?' asked Al, his pale eyes glinting.

'I'm gonna see what makes Holbrook tick. And see if I can find out why the town leaders here won't fight back.'

Silas Henry became conscious during the week Matt lay recovering following his own beating. Weak and confused at first, the old man talked some. But it was a day later before he was strong enough to relate what he recalled happening to him.

'Two-finger Buck, Holbrook's gorilla, came to the stables an' told me that since I had refused to pay any more protection money, the boss had told him to teach me a lesson. Lance Rainey stood by an' watched. I remember his face the last thing I saw before I blacked out.'

'Why doesn't the town council get together and do something about the situation?' Matt asked.

The faded old eyes glared at him and Silas snorted.

''Cause they're all afeered of gettin' jist what I got. Holbrook's got 'em scared outta their pants. They won't buck him.'

'What if they hired a town marshal who would make a few changes in the way things are going?'

Silas turned his head and squinted at Matt.

'You offerin' to do the job?' he asked, his

old eyes measuring the young man sitting across the room from him.

'Maybe.'

'Do you think you're bigger than Holbrook an' his whole bunch of cutthroats?'

'Maybe,' Matt said again. 'Maybe a sawed off double barreled shotgun and me could do the job.'

'That's a lotta maybes. Holbrook an' his gang won't stop at nothin' to get what he wants.' Silas squinted at Matt. 'However, why don't I try to get the town council together, quiet-like, up here in my place. You can tell them what you have in mind.'

Matt thought about it for a long minute, turning over what had come to him since he had talked with Emmy about the happenings in Rimrock. He nodded.

'Why don't we do that? They can mull it over among themselves and decide if they want to try it.'

Al Rooney was about to leave the hotel when Emmy stopped him in the lobby.

'Al, I heard Matt tell you to look up some help. There's a young man on the porch who just asked me if there were any ranches about that were looking for hands. I couldn't help him, but maybe you would want talk with him. He might be able to help you.'

Al nodded. 'Thank you, Miss Emmy. I'll sound him out.' He nodded again to her, turned and walked out of the hotel. He paused on the porch. He stood quietly for a moment, slowly eyeing movement on the main street. His eyes eventually saw the man Emmy had mentioned, leaning against a porch post, his eyes taking in those who walked by.

Al turned to him. 'Miss Emmy, the lady in the hotel said you was lookin' for a job. That right?'

He was young. Still in early twenties, thought Rooney. And he wore no gun. His face was clean-shaven, except for a small mustache, his eyes sharp-blue and keen. He looked at Rooney as he spoke.

'Yeah. I'm sorta out of a job. Come up from the border, thinkin' maybe I could catch on to a ranch somewhere along the way. So far I ain't had no luck.'

Al eyed him keenly. 'I'm Al Rooney and the foreman of a small hoss ranch nearby. What's your moniker?'

The young man hesitated and then nodded. 'Obliged to know you. I'm Bill. Bill Smith.'

There seemed to be a lot of 'Bill Smiths' around since the war, mused Al Rooney. Who may have fought on either side of the conflict.

'Y'all know anything about horses?'

Smith nodded. 'Yeah. I've rode a few. Some of 'em purty rough, but I stayed with 'em.'

Rooney decided to see what the young man could do. A few days with taming those rowdy horses, smoothing them out before selling to the army, would tell him what kind of mettle the man was made of. He nodded.

'My outfit's about five miles outta town, east.' He nodded the direction. 'You got a hoss?'

Smith shook his head. 'My hoss broke a leg about ten miles outta town. I had to shoot him. I caught a ride with a farmer and got my gear all here in his wagon. It's over to the livery.'

Al nodded. 'All right. You had breakfast?'

Smith shook his head.

'Go in an' have Emmy fix you a good meal. Then go over to the livery an' hire a hoss to ride out to the ranch. We lost a partner recently an' you kin have his hoss, or break one of the cayuses out of our herd. Your pay starts right now.' He reached into a pocket and pulled out several silver dollars. 'This'll do you 'til you talk over terms with the boss.'

Al left as the young man eagerly entered the hotel dining-room for a meal. There were things to be done in town, provisions to be bought, and a final talk with Matt before he returned to the ranch. He reasoned that Smith would be there before him.

Lear Holbrook was livid. His foreman had come in from the basin, where he had found Olly and Slag all tied up and the horses gone from the holding canyon. Wilson had just finished burying the hand Al had shot.

'You mean to tell me that one skinny old wrangler over-powered three of you, killed one, tied you up and got away with two hundred horses? That is unbelievable, and for me, inexcusable.'

'Not when it is Al Rooney,' Rainey hissed from his usual place in the corner chair.

Holbrook paid no attention to him. He continued railing at Wilson, who stood before him, red-faced and angry at the invective being thrown at him.

Finally the saloon-owner and town boss slowly quieted down and fell silent. He motioned Wilson to a seat and sat back in his chair, frowning, his face sullen in thought. It was several minutes before he stirred.

He glanced over at Lance Rainey.

'What was it you was sayin' about that old puncher what held a gun on us the other day?'

'If he's who I think he is, he's a shootist,' Lance said. 'I knew about him a long time ago. He rode with Quantrill in '63. He was high up in Quantrill's favor. He's got plenty of notches on his gun.'

'He's pushin' the years, then,' muttered Wilson.

'Not necessarily,' Holbrook shook his head. 'That wasn't so long ago. However, he's one to look out for. From what I see, Curtis is no gunman. He's gotta be took out of the way.' He looked at Rainey.

'You do it! Make up an excuse of some kind and make him go for his gun. If you are as fast as you let on to be, he won't be any trouble.'

'I may have to take out Al Rooney first,' Rainey hissed. 'He's the one I'm leery of.'

Holbrook shrugged. 'Whatever, do it.' He turned to Tip Wilson. 'Take three or four boys and go out and round up them horses again and this time, drive them right to the ranch. I'll be finding a buyer for them.'

'That's hoss-stealin', boss,' Wilson growled. 'A feller can get hisself hung doin' that.'

'You let me handle it. We're rounding up a bunch of wild broncs on my land and getting rid of them. You just get the job done.'

It was three weeks before Matt mounted a horse. Even then he felt a twinge as he swung over the saddle. Emmy watched from the porch and saw his mouth twist with the pain. She shook her head.

'Hard-headed man,' she scolded. 'Another week wouldn't make any difference in those horses. And it would give your ribs a little longer to heal.'

He grinned at her. 'A little pain is just part of living, Emmy. See you tomorrow. Tell your dad I will be back in time for the meeting.' He touched the brim of his hat with a forefinger, turned his horse and rode away. She watched him go with a tender look upon her face. Emmy Henry knew her heart had gone to the tall, handsome young man. And suddenly she was happy, a song seeming to spring from her heart.

It was mid-afternoon when Matt came to

the old cabin in the basin and found Al Rooney waiting there.

'I thought you'd be along afore long,' the older man said, as Matt dismounted and led the horse to the creek to drink. As the animal satisfied himself with the cool, flowing water, Al brought Matt up to date on his activities.

'The hosses are about six miles over.' He pointed toward the towering ledge of the red mesa that formed the north rim of the basin. 'That's a big meadow in a box canyon, with water and only one way in or out. Thar's enough graze fer about a month. I figured you'd have things settled one way or t'other by then. I found two men wantin' work. One of them is the kid, Bill Smith.' His lips twisted into a wry smile as he spoke the name. 'Seems to be a lot of Bill Smiths around these days. I've got them takin' turns at night, guardin' the hosses.'

Matt gazed out over the gentle undulations of the basin, noting the lush midsummer graze, the corpse of live oak, aspen, pine and piñon, all under the wide, blue expanse of the open sky.

In the distance an eagle floated high above the basin, its eyes searching for the unwary rodent that would make a meal for hungry young in a cliff-hung nest. Buzzards circled nearby, narrowing in on something dead in the center of the basin. All this Matt's keen eyes took in with a deep satisfaction.

He shook his shoulders and let out a deep breath.

'It's all worth fighting for, Al. And we're going to give it our best. Somehow, we've got to find out what there is about the basin that makes Holbrook want it so bad.'

Al nodded. He rolled a cigarette and bent to strike a match on a boot-heel.

'We'll find it, pardner … we'll find it all right.'

CHAPTER NINE

Silas Henry, owner of the hotel and the attached eatery, moved carefully about his apartment, as he talked with Rimrock's mayor, Mose Guthrie.

'We've got to do something about Holbrook.' His eyes narrowed at the mayor. 'It can't go on like this. The town is taken by an unruly crowd, who answers only to Holbrook.' Then he proceeded to tell the mayor about Matt Curtis and the possibility that the young rancher might help the town out with its problems.

Mose Guthrie had been mayor of Rimrock for several years. Each time the election came around Mose threw his hat into the ring, since no one else seemed interested in the fifty-dollar-a-month job which carried little with it, little duty to perform and very little prestige.

Once he had studied law, but he had never taken on the grueling tasks of defending or prosecuting, creating writs, facing overworked, irascible judges, drawing up wills and arbitrating between two ranchers squared off at each other over a bull calf with a blotched brand. The job of mayor in the small town of Rimrock suited him and he clung to it year by year, hoping no one else would ever contest him come election time.

The mayor listened to Si Henry, who was now up and moving carefully about his apartment on the second floor of the hotel. His expression was stoic as he listened, his eyes fastened on the liveryman pacing about the room as he talked. At last he interrupted.

'What do you know about this fellow, Curtis? Other than what you see and what he tells you?'

Silas Henry looked at him for a long moment.

'I know he is the only person who has come up with any kind of plan to get the town out of this mess. And a mess we got ourselves into.'

'Be that as it may, it is mightily risky.'

'Most things are when you deal with money and power,' Si answered testily. 'Well, what about it? Will you get the council together?'

'What has Curtis got to gain out of this?'

asked the mayor. 'He isn't a citizen of Rimrock. Why should he put himself out for us?'

'I told you,' said Si bluntly. 'Lear Holbrook's men attacked his camp and killed his partner. Then they run off his horses. I reckon he's got a pretty good stake in what needs to be done about Holbrook and his gang.'

The mayor sat lost in thought for several minutes. Silas brought each of them a cup of coffee. Eventually Mose spoke.

'It'll have to be kept real quiet,' he said. 'But I'll get most of the council together. I'll bring just the ones I can trust, in fact.' He raised his heavy eyes to the liveryman. 'God Almighty help us, if it leaks out to Holbrook what we're talking about.'

Al Rooney and Matt loped through the basin to where the horses were herded into and held in a large meadow. Matt nodded, pleased at the sight of the animals grazing in knee-deep grass and on seeing the small creek that flowed through one side of the meadow.

He met and shook hands with the two men hired by Al Rooney to help with the horses.

'You all stay with us, and we'll have us a

horse ranch here one day that will be the talk of the territory,' he told them. Both men seemed satisfied with the job. Matt eyed the young man, Bill Smith, carefully. In his early twenties, Matt surmised. Wearing a sixgun on his right hip. He eyed Matt carefully, his eyes cool.

'I don't take to the likes of Holbrook and them he has around him,' the older man, Jed Fellows, said in a soft, Texan drawl. 'This kind of job suits me jist fine.'

Matt sized him up as one who would stand in a fight. The young man, Smith, would be judged after some incident that proved his worth. One thing was for certain, if they stayed on, there was little doubt of having further brushes with trouble, with Holbrook wanting the basin. The time would come when their loyalty to the spread was tested.

Matt spent most of the day with the horse herd. At mid-afternoon he and Al rode back to the old cabin by the creek. Matt sat looking at the site.

'I'll tear down that old cabin,' he mused to Al. 'Maybe move back a little further from the creek to be safe from flash floods off the mesa, and build a nice place, one that will last a while.'

'Got your eyes on a filly, eh?' Al grinned at him. Matt shrugged and smiled wryly.

'All in good time, my friend. There's one around for every man, if he looks long enough.'

'It appears like you've already looked and got hooked a little.' Al chuckled. Matt did not answer, but Al noticed the edges of his ears become somewhat red.

Tip Wilson, the foreman of the LH spread, with five men from the ranch, entered the basin and spread out, looking for the horses.

They came together several hours following their starting of the search, all admitting they had found no animals.

'Found Jack's hoss out thar, just over by the mesa slope,' one of the men said. 'But I didn't see hide ner hair of any of that herd we had penned up.'

Wilson rolled a cigarette and smoked, drawing in deeply and letting the smoke out slowly. They had dismounted and were squatting or standing in the shade of a huge live oak, not far from the old cabin. Several of the men took advantage of the lull in activity to stretch out and take a long drink from the clear water of the creek a few yards away.

'All right.' Wilson stirred and spoke to the men. 'Tracks don't say the hosses was drove from the basin, so they're in here somewhere. Likely in a meadow or canyon, jist like we had 'em before, only a different place. Spread out and search the slopes of the mesa. Look in all the canyons, draws and arroyos. Whoever finds 'em, fire three shots. We'll all gather on him.'

It was coming on dusk when the rolling echoes of three shots from a sixgun reached across the basin. The slopes of the mesa turned from red to pink, slowly darkening to blue and purple as the sun lowered its orange disk below the rim.

The LH men gathered on the one who had fired the shots. They were near the far edge of the mesa, where a small canyon mouth opened into the basin.

'They're back in there,' the cowboy said. 'I saw tracks and then drifted back to where I could see. The break there opens up to a big meadow.'

'How many wranglers?' Tip Wilson asked.

'I seen two men, but a'course there could've been more.'

'Probably are more,' mused Wilson. 'All right. Let's back off and we'll decide what has to be done.'

'I know what has to be done,' one of the men groused. 'We gotta go in thar, take chances on gettin' ourselves shot up.'

Wilson nodded. 'Yep, you got it. Maybe a scratch er two. How we're gonna do it, is what we gotta think out. Come on, let's go, afore one of them wranglers sees us.'

Mayor Mose Guthrie, with six other leading citizens of Rimrock met in the apartment of Silas and Emmy Henry. The young woman busied herself pouring coffee and placed a plate of doughnuts on a small table in their living-room. She excused herself and went into the kitchen, closing the door behind her.

Emmy knew what the conversation was to be about. Silas had told her about the talk he had had with Matt Curtis. She was fearful of the decision the town fathers would make. They were angry and afraid of Lear Holbrook and his men. They would grasp at any chance of getting from under his power. She did not doubt that they would not hesitate to use Matt as their buffer. Just so long as they did not endanger themselves.

She was worried that Matt had not as yet made his appearance for the meeting, as he had said he would. She had just settled herself with some sewing when he knocked upon the door.

As she opened it her smile enveloped him. He removed his hat and reaching out touched her hand. Her heart leaped in her chest and her face flushed.

'They are in the living-room, Matt.' She spoke softly as she took his hat. 'I was beginning to worry about you.'

He smiled at her. 'It is nice to be worried about by such a beautiful lady,' he told her, his eyes searching her features. His own heart was giving him signs that this young woman was returning his own signals. Suddenly he knew that Emmy Henry was his to love and to hold, if he spoke the word.

She touched his arm and lowered her eyes.

'In there.' She nodded toward the next room. 'They are waiting for you.' She looked him directly in the eyes then and said softly, 'Be careful.'

She drew a deep, shuddering breath as he walked into the other room. Her full breasts swelled and tingled as she thought of things a nice young woman was not supposed to think about. But, after all, who can control their thoughts when they are in love? she thought.

Silas Henry nodded to Matt as he entered the room.

'Here he is, just like he said he would be,' he said. Quickly he made introductions around the room. Hard eyes, inquisitive eyes, and somewhat questioning, fearful eyes, with short nods, acknowledged the introductions.

The mayor eyed Matt severely, an expensive cigar screwed between tightly compressed lips. His look was cold, unbelieving. Matt's eyes met those of the mayor's scrutiny levelly, without wavering.

'What advice can you give us, Mr Curtis,' asked the mayor, his tone cynical, 'that will help us with our problem?'

Matt returned his gaze for a long moment. The same question seemed to be on every face in the room.

'Get rid of Lear Holbrook and his gang, and take your town back,' Matt said quietly, in soft, carrying tones.

'Oh, yes. Just like that,' said the mayor, wryly. 'We just say, get out and they get. Just like that.' He gave a short, derisive laugh.

'Fire the marshal and hire one who will make your town ordinances stick. Throw some of them in jail and keep them there until they give in. Lead them to the town limits and kick them out and advise them to never return.'

He looked into the other faces. Tom Clogg, recently recovered from a severe beating at the hands of Two-finger Buck and his cohorts; Arnold Matthews, owner of the town saddlery; Silas Henry, the liveryman, all had known the heavy fists of Holbrook's bullies. Every man looking at him was paying increasing blackmail, to the very man who set the fists against them.

'It's easier said than done,' grunted Jake Forrest, owner of the small saloon at the north end of town. His operation was for the lesser affluent members of Rimrock society, to enjoy the services of several women of questionable repute who piled their ancient trade out of his establishment. Lear Holbrook not only levied protection fees against the saloonkeeper, but also forced each of the women to turn over half of their earnings to him.

'Every time you pay him protection money, he is into you a little deeper. True, to give him such an ultimatum will make him blow up. But if you hire a marshal that ain't afraid of Holbrook an' his men, an' give him back-up, before long you'll have your town back.'

'Where would we find such a feller, even if we wanted to hire him?' asked Tom Clogg.

Matt looked at each of them stoically. His voice was low and cold when he spoke.

'Holbrook's men, led by Two-finger Buck, gave me a taste of what some of you have experienced. Holbrook an' his rannies stole my horse herd. I got them back, but can't do anything about developing my holdings in the basin because of his pressure. Right now I have men tied up doing nothing but guarding my herd. So I do have a card in this game.'

They looked at him, some in disdain, the mayor with a cynical glare.

Silas Henry eyed Matt levelly and then spoke.

'Are you offerin' to take on the job of marshal in Rimrock?'

Matt took makings from a pocket and slowly built a cigarette. Every eye in the room was on the movement of his fingers. He twisted the end, put the cigarette between his lips, lighted it with a kitchen match and inhaled. He blew the smoke from his lungs.

He nodded. 'Yes,' he said softly. 'I'll take the job. But only if I can do it my way.'

The men looked at him askance, some shaking their heads. But when a vote was taken, there was a majority of hands raised, giving Matt the job as marshal of Rimrock.

CHAPTER TEN

'Here they come!' Al Rooney called softly over his shoulder to the Texan, Jed Fellows, who crouched behind a large boulder, several yards from the trail leading into the meadow. The young man, Bill Smith, was equally well hidden, at the side of the trail. Al, on guard for the early shift until midnight, had heard the jingle of a spur chain, alerting him to the attack.

Tip Wilson had reconnoitered the entrance to the meadow himself as soon as it had become dark. The moon was only a thin sliver, waning toward change and would cast no light of any significance. He had seen the camp-fire of the horse guards and already knew there were only three men. He decided that with his six men and himself they would be able to surprise the wranglers and take the horses with little or no battle.

'All right,' he instructed his men. 'Three of you take the left side of the trail. The others follow me on the right. No talkin'. We oughta be able to surprise 'em.'

Cautious as they might be, it was impossible for seven men to advance though almost total darkness, in unfamiliar terrain, without making some noise. Spurs were removed, but boot-heels, used to locking into stirrups, skidded on stones, gun belts creaked, and the deep breathing of walking men, all combined to create noises un-intended, but discernible to the listener.

Al Rooney located their attackers when they were fifty yards along the trail into the meadow. He passed the word back to wait for his signal. He had already cocked his Winchester .44, so the initial 'click' of the cocking mechanism would not betray his location. His keen eyes picked up dim, dark shadows, slowly moving against the lighter night darkness of the trail. He let the attackers come closer, the shadows now clearer. Leveling his rifle, he centered on the leading figure and squeezed the trigger.

The blast of the rifle, the flash of the muzzle, was the signal for Al's men to begin firing in the same direction. The men did just that, their rifles and sixguns pouring a rain of hot lead down the dark trail.

'Get 'em, boys!' Tip Wilson roared, his sixgun in his hand and blasting. He got away one shot, then a blow slammed into his left leg. He fell heavily, cursing, to the ground. There was a cry behind him as another of his men was hit. The attackers paused momentarily and then pressed on, emptying their weapons at the muzzle-flashes they saw before them. But the defenders were too powerful, the fire too heavy. When another of their group fell, the remainder slowly retreated, leaving one dead, their leader, Tip Wilson, seriously wounded, and supporting another man one with a chest wound.

When the returning fire ceased, Al Rooney yelled for the defenders of the meadow to hold fire.

'I think they're gone,' Jed Fellows said. He rose cautiously and peered into the darkness. 'I heard hosses runnin'. They're gone.'

'Well, some of 'em was hurt.' Bill Smith appeared at Rooney's side. The men came in and stood about Rooney. As they stood there, a voice called out from the trail.

'Come and get me, men. Don't leave me here to bleed to death, for Gawd's sake.'

Rooney nudged Fellows. 'They run off and left one of their boys out there. Reckon we'd better see about him.'

'Aw, Al, you go up to 'im an' he'll probably shoot you jist for the pure meanness of it,'

Bill Smith said, his young face still tense after the quick fight.

'You all go back to the fire an' get it started again,' Al ordered the men. 'Jed, you come with me an' we'll just see how bad this ranny is shot.'

Al and Jed, with guns drawn moved slowly and cautiously down the trail. Al paused, motioning Jed to stop. Heavy breathing told him the wounded man was close by.

'Speak up, buddy. We don't want to hurt you any more than you are. Maybe we can help,' Al said quietly into the darkness.

'My leg is shot bad,' Tip Wilson said hoarsely from where he lay. 'I'm bleedin' real bad an' I cain't seem to get...' He groaned and was silent.

Following the sound of his voice, Al and Jed found him. Carefully bending over him, Al saw he was now unarmed and was unconscious. He straightened.

'Let's tote 'em over to the fire,' he said to Jed. 'Maybe we can bind 'em up an' stop the bleedin'. I ain't got much sympathy for someone who stands in the dark an' takes pop-shots at me, but I won't let a dawg bleed to death, iff'n I can help it.'

'Here, let me get him. You steady him when I heave him on my shoulders.' Jed bent over, seized Wilson, who was no small man, and lifted him to his shoulders. Al helped to settle the inert body in his grasp.

Back at the fire Al motioned for Bill Smith to gather more wood.

'Take a walk back along the trail an' see if you find any more wounded back there. Be careful.'

Smith nodded, added more fuel to the fire, then disappeared into the darkness.

Jed laid Wilson's unconscious body beside the fire, which was beginning to flame again with the dried branches tossed on the glowing embers. Al knelt beside the man and, with his knife, slit the pant leg where blood continued to darken the cloth. He examined the wound carefully.

'Waal, it looks like he was lucky,' he told Jed. 'The bullet went through the muscle an' meat an' didn't hit any bone. We'll wrap him up good an' one of us'll take him into Rimrock to the sawbones. I don't think we're gonna have any more visitors from Holbrook's bunch. Not tonight, at least.'

The man sent to look for other wounded LH men, came back to the fire.

'There's a dead one back there, Al. One of us got him plumb center atween the eyes.'

'You and Smith go get him. We'll take 'em

both into town tomorrow and leave 'em with the doctor an' undertaker. Holbrook keeps this up he's goin' to run outta men to work his spread.'

It was the morning after the town council had met, some of them reluctantly, and had hired Matt Curtis as marshal of Rimrock. Matt left his boarding-house room and ate breakfast in the hotel restaurant. Emmy Henry served him his coffee and ham and eggs. She was somewhat pale and her hands trembled as she placed his coffee cup on the table.

'Is something the matter?' Matt asked, his eyes taking in the dark circles under her eyes.

She was silent a long moment.

'I ... I just wish you hadn't taken the job as marshal. I'm afraid you'll get hurt. Hurt bad. And ... I just couldn't stand it!' She sobbed and ran from the dining-room. Two other tables were filled with patrons and they eyed Matt with sidelong glances, wondering what the handsome ranny had said to make the waitress cry and leave the room.

Matt left the restaurant. Leaning against a hotel porch post, he rolled a cigarette and inhaled deeply, letting the smoke trickle from his lips. Then, finishing his smoke, he stepped out on the boardwalk and walked toward the town marshal's office. He paused for a moment, then shoved the door open and walked into the office.

Willie Williams was the deputy appointed by Holbrook without the permission of the town council. He was slovenly, shaved at most once a week and bathed sometime. The office stank of stale tobacco, whiskey-breath and body-odor. Williams sat with scuffed boots up on the desk, leaning back, half-asleep, in the chair back of the spur-scarred piece of furniture.

He rolled a bleary eye at Matt.

'What do you want? Bustin' in my office like you owned it,' he grunted.

'Phew, this place stinks,' Matt said, wrinkling his nose. He reached back of him and opened the outer door wide. 'Let some air in here.'

Williams straightened and brought his feet down. 'Just who do you think you are? This is my office and I want the door shut.'

'You are wrong on two counts, Willie,' said Matt. He reached over and seized the tarnished silver marshal's badge on Williams's shirt. He jerked it loose and slipped it into his shirt pocket.

'This is *my* office now, and the door stays open.' He walked over to the gun rack on the opposite wall, which held three rifles, a single-barreled shotgun, and a double-barreled, sawn-off, .10 gauge shotgun.

He took the double-barreled shotgun from the rack, broke it open and peered through the barrel.

'Like everything else in this dump, it's dirty.' He tucked it under his arm and took a handful of shells from a box on a shelf beneath the rack. He slipped two into the empty chambers of the shotgun. He snapped the barrels shut with a 'clunk' and looked at Williams.

'I'm the marshal of Rimrock by appointment of the town council.' He pointed the shotgun at Williams. 'Get up and get into that cell, there.' He gestured with the gun toward one of the two empty cells at the end of the room.

'You can't...'

Matt cocked one barrel of the gun and looked at Williams, his eyes glinting. The former deputy rose, walked to one of the cells, opened the door and went inside, shutting the door after him. Matt took a set of keys from a nail on the wall back of the desk and unhurriedly locked the cell door.

'This is so I can make a call on Holbrook without your gettin' there before me with certain news I have for him,' Matt said, grinning with a cold glint of teeth at Williams. 'I'll be back whenever I get time.'

Matt returned the keys to the nail and paused. He leaned the shotgun against the desk, removed his sixgun from its holster and checked the cylinder to make certain each chamber was filled. Satisfied all was in order, he tugged his hat lower over his eyes and stepped from the door of the office.

Two-finger Buck stood looking at him, a puzzled expression on his face. With him were the two roustabouts who had held Matt while Buck worked him over.

Matt swung the shotgun around to cover the three.

'Well, now, howdy men. You're just the three I wanted to see first, after being appointed marshal of this here town.'

Buck stared at him and then threw back his shaggy head and laughed.

'Boys, I guess we didn't do a good enough job on this ranny. Com'on, let's give him another lesson. Only make this one a good one–'

He stopped laughing and backed up

abruptly as Matt drew back both hammers of the shotgun.

'Now, you three boys, just come on in. There's a little room in there that will be just right for you. Come on!' He gestured with the gun and the two with Two-finger Buck hurried into the jail, with their big companion trailing reluctantly to bring up the rear.

Matt opened the cell door and motioned for the two to go on in. As Buck stepped up to the door, Matt spoke.

'Not you, Buck. I want to have a little talk with you first. Set down in that chair yonder until I get these lads comfortable.'

Buck settled into the chair before the desk, his little eyes, red and mean, half-buried in his moon-face, noting Matt's every move. Buck was huge. Six feet four and weighing in at about 250 pounds. His body was encased in a thick layer of fat, but under the fat were huge, latent muscles. He had depended upon his size for many years to intimidate and overpower opponents.

Matt, on the other hand, was slightly over six feet, weighing in the neighborhood of 170 pounds. He was tough and strong from the years of ranch work and meeting the challenge of Western living. He had held his own in the rough and tumble camp-fire wrestling and scraping for years and, more often than not, had come out the winner.

The two hardcases entered the cell sullenly, one sneering at Matt.

'You're one waddie that's gonna get his rope busted real quick,' he said. 'You'd better put Buck in here and take on us two, instead of him.'

'I'm thinking about it,' Matt said. He locked the door and turned to the hulk who was sitting and smirking at him.

Buck, still smirking, rose. As he did so, Matt swung the shotgun by the barrel. The stock, hardened over years, crashed into Buck's jaw. The huge man yelled, his eyes rolled back into his head, and he slumped back into the chair, blood dripping from his mouth. Two-finger was out cold.

'I don't take chances with rabid skunks,' Matt gritted, staring at Buck's friends in the cell. He unlocked the cell door and motioned for the two men to come out. 'Come on out an' drag your pard in there. You,' he pointed to one, 'what's your moniker?'

'Lute,' the man said, eyeing Matt warily.

'Lute, you an' your buddy come out here and help drag him in there.' His cold eyes narrowed.

'Now, Marshal, I was jest doin' what Buck paid me to do when we beat on you–'

'Just do as I tell you and we'll get along fine.' Matt motioned again for the two men to come out of the cell. Watching Matt from the corners of their eyes, the men seized Buck by the arms and legs, and staggered with him into the cell. There they dumped him unceremoniously on the floor and turned to Matt. Matt motioned with a forefinger at Lute.

'Now, you come on out. Let's see how you do just by yourself.'

Lute grinned and winked at his companion.

'This here is Sam, since you ain't been properly interduced,' he said. With a rush he came out of the cell, fists flailing, with Sam behind him. Lute skidded to a halt and began to circle to Matt's right, while Sam sidled around to the left. Matt watched both as they moved about him.

When Matt backed up against the desk, Lute rushed him. A large, rope-hardened fist met him in the belly. He bent double, gasping for breath, to meet a knee coming up that slammed into his face. Lute screamed in pain and fell back to the floor, holding his crushed and bleeding nose and mouth.

Sam launched himself across the desk, to meet thin air as Matt sidestepped. As Sam slid by him, Matt punched him solidly in the kidneys and as he yelled and slid off the desk onto the floor, Matt seized him. He pushed him back against the cell and slammed a straight right to his jaw. Sam melted and joined his companion on the floor.

Matt took a deep breath. He seized both men by their shirt collars and dragged them into the cell with Two-finger Buck. He locked the door on them, righted the desk chair that had fallen over during the fracas, and rolled himself a cigarette. He drew in a deep breath, then let the smoke trickle out of his mouth. He relaxed.

'You are some ring-tailed foot-stomper when you get riled up, you are,' the former deputy said from his cell. 'But them three ain't nothin'. You gotta face Holbrook an' that hissin' Rainey yet.'

Matt nodded. 'I know.' He finished the smoke and ground it out on the dirty office floor. 'I might as well get to it,' he said. He rose, took the shotgun and moved to the door. He looked back at the man in the cell whose job he had just taken over. 'Why don't you just stay put for a while? Just while I go have a little confab with your boss.'

Williams grinned and spread himself on the bunk.

'I ain't goin' nowhere, Marshal Curtis. I'm right comfortable where I am.'

Cradling the shotgun in his arms, Matt stepped from the door of the jail and paused, looking first one way and the other at the main street of the town.

As he did so, Al Rooney came into sight at the far end of the street, herding Tip Wilson before him, who rode painfully on his horse, favoring his wounded leg. Rooney led another horse across which was draped the inert body of the cowhand killed in the night raid on the basin.

Matt let out a gust of air.

'Looks like trouble in this place is like grapes. It comes in bunches.'

CHAPTER ELEVEN

Rooney reined up before the rail and leaning on his saddle horn, looked down at Matt.

'Waal, I see you're comin' up in the world, er goin' the other way. Is that silver star there meanin' what it usually means?'

'Yep,' said Matt. 'Duly appointed by the town council and all wrote up legal-like by the town mayor hisself.'

'Then I got business fer you. This feller,' Al jerked a thumb at Tip Wilson, 'tried to run off your horses again. That one,' he pointed to the body draped across the saddle of the horse he was leading, 'he was in the fracas an' didn't make it. There's another one or two around somewheres that caught some lead.'

Matt walked over to Wilson and looked at the leg.

'You'll need Doc Marcus to look at that. Come on in and I'll send for him.' He helped Wilson out of the saddle and led him into the office. 'Al, you take the body down to the undertaker's, and then find the doctor and send him along. Come on back, then, and tell me what went on out there.'

'Stretch out there on that cot.' Matt pointed to a small bunk used by the deputy when it was necessary for him to spend the night in the jail office. Wilson did as he was directed willingly, wincing as he settled down on the blankets. From the main cell Williams called to him.

'How'd it go out there yesterday?' he asked Wilson. 'Did you get this feller's hosses again?'

'We got shot up pretty bad, was what happened,' grunted Wilson. 'I'm beginnin' to think I'm tryin' to head up the wrong spread.'

'You just might ponder on that awhile,' Matt told him. 'I'm filed on the basin proper, besides, I have a deed to the land around three of the springs. I'm going to make me a horse ranch out there, and you'd be wise to go back to your ranch and let me be.'

Wilson eyed him levelly.

'Curtis, if I thought for one minute I was bein' put in the way of bein' called a hoss-thief, I'd quit the LH spread. But the way it's been told to me, *you're* the one tryin' take land that ain't yours to take.'

'Your boss is trying to take something that ain't *his* to take, Wilson. There's something else behind his wanting the basin bad enough to steal and kill for it. Do you know what it might be?'

Wilson shook his head, but had started to answer, when the doctor came bustling into the room, carrying his black bag and trailed by Al Rooney.

'Who's hurt?' he asked. Then he saw Tip Wilson stretched out on the cot. In a few moments, with Matt's help, he had Wilson's clothes off and his underwear opened to where he could examine the wound.

'The round went in and out of the meaty muscles there, in the thigh,' he commented. He poked and probed while Wilson tensed and swore at the pain.

'Dognap it, Doc, you're rough,' he said through gritted teeth. 'That hurts.'

'Don't hurt near as much as it would if I had to saw that leg off,' the old doctor grunted. He treated the wound with liniment and then a salve and bound it tightly with bandages. 'You come and see me in a day or two and I'll change the bandage. And you stay off the leg in the meantime. No walking around and no horse-riding.'

'But, Doc–' Wilson began and was interrupted by Matt. 'He'll be quiet for a spell, Doctor,' Matt said with a glint in his eyes. 'That cell right there will be real nice for him to rest up in.' Matt motioned for Williams. 'The door ain't locked, Williams. You help Wilson to the bunk and you're free to go. Just stay away from the Rimrock saloon, hear?'

Williams did as he was ordered, then slipped out of the door. Rooney looked questioningly at Matt.

Matt shrugged. 'Maybe it's just as well. I'll tend to Holbrook after Doc sees to old Two-finger Buck in there.' He nodded to the cell opposite the one being occupied by Tip Wilson.

'You've been busy,' grunted the doctor. 'How long you been marshal? And you've banged up three of Holbrook's hoodlums and your friend there has shot up others of his cowhands.'

'Just doing my duty, Doc,' Matt said drily. 'You take a look at those three jaspers and I'll be on my way. Al, you hang around and lock the cell after the doctor leaves.'

Al shrugged and drew up a chair, yawning as he did so.

'Don't mind if I do,' he said. 'Ain't had

much sleep the last three or four nights.'

Williams came in the back door of the saloon as Matt walked through the swinging doors off the front boardwalk. The swamper, a crippled, retired cowhand who had been stomped by a wild bronc, was sweeping and mopping the floor.

Matt gestured with the shotgun.

'Williams, just go back out to where you came from. You've no business here at the moment.'

Williams turned and, without argument, departed swiftly through the door through which he had just come. Matt spoke to the swampy.

'Where's the bartender?'

'He don't come in 'til ten o'clock,' the man said. Matt nodded.

'You go right ahead with your work,' Matt said. 'It's probably the only honest work being done around this place.' The old-timer grinned and returned to his swamping.

Matt walked to the back of the saloon, to the door leading into Holbrook's office. He heard the hoarse sound of men's voices and paused a moment. The words were not audible through the thick door.

Matt seized the knob, turned it and shoved

the door open, allowing it to slam back against the office wall. He stepped through the doorway and faced Lear Holbrook across the desk.

'What in–'

'Seems like I've been here before, Mr Holbrook. Only this time I come bearing orders from the town council.'

'Rainey, throw this *hombre* out of here, right now!' Holbrook leaped to his feet in rage, dropping his cigar in the process.

His bodyguard sprang to his feet, his hand flashing down to fasten upon his gun butts. It froze there. The shotgun in Matt's hand swung to point its black, evil bores at Holbrook's belly, and the dual hammers drew back with an ominous click.

'Go right ahead, Rainey,' Matt said, never taking his eyes off the saloon-owner. 'But when you fire, I release double barrels of deer slugs into your boss's belly. He'll be dead and you'll be out of a job and up for murdering a duly appointed marshal of the law.'

'Where's Williams?' yelled Holbrook. 'You ain't no marshal. I never gave you the job as marshal.'

'Nope. And you ain't throwing me out of the job, neither. Now, both of you sit and listen–'

'Kill him, Rainey! I order you, shoot him!' yelled Holbrook, his face almost black with rage. His hands trembled and saliva sprayed from his thick lips.

'Sure he will, Holbrook. And when he draws, I fill you full of slugs from this double-barrel. Now, both of you, *sit down!*'

Rainey hissed in his anger, his eyes shooting sparks, but settled back into his chair, his hands on his thighs, but only a flick away from his gun.

Holbrook dropped back into his chair and sat trembling, glaring at Matt.

'Now, both of you listen, and listen good. The town council has given me the job as marshal. Williams is out. The first thing we are going to do, Holbrook, is to cease this protection scheme of yours. Your gang of gunnies is no longer in control. Send them back to your ranch, fire them, do whatever you want to do with them. But, get them out of town.'

'Do you think you can buck me and twenty men on my payroll?' sneered Holbrook. He was beginning to settle his anger now, and watched Matt's every move. 'One man against a gang? How long do you think you'll last?'

'Just as long as it takes me to pull this

trigger, Holbrook. From now on I'm your shadow. By the way, three of your thugs are in jail for interfering with the law. Your foreman, Wilson, is also there, being worked on by Doc Marcus right now. Wilson got a slug in the leg, leading your waddies against my crew, trying to get at my horses again. And,' he drew a deep breath and let his anger show, 'my man killed another of your cowhands in the fracas.'

'You killed another of my hands? I'll have the sheriff after you! I've already sent for him,' stormed Holbrook.

'You won't do nothing. You come with me, right now, over to the bank.'

Holbrook leaned back in his chair.

'Just what do you want me at the bank for?' he asked.

Matt Curtis gestured with the cocked shotgun, and Holbrook winced.

'Come and see,' Matt said wryly. 'And Rainey, you drop your gun and come along with us.'

CHAPTER TWELVE

Roscoe Warren, in Laramie, received Lear Holbrook's telegram from the hand of a roustabout sent from the telegraph office. He sat on the side of his bed and rubbed his face, now stubbly with a day-old beard. He smacked his lips and winced at the taste of stale tobacco, beer and whiskey, indulged in the evening before.

He was the sheriff of Rimrock, appointed by Lear Holbrook and paid by him, one hundred a month, a room in Holbrook's hotel, and meals at the hotel restaurant. The man from the telegraph office had awakened him. Bleary-eyed, he unfolded the telegram and peered at it.

Swearing and muttering to himself, he tossed the paper on the bed and, staggering over to the washstand, sloshed in a bowlful of water from the pitcher, and splashed his face. He wiped himself on the towel hanging close by from a hook on the stand, then returned to the bed. Seating himself with a grunt, he picked up the telegram.

Lear Holbrook ordered him to cease whatever he was doing and return to Rimrock on the next stage. The town boss gave no reason. Just gave the order, expecting it to be obeyed forthwith and without question.

Normally there would have been no question of instant obedience. However, this order came at a time when Sheriff Warren was deeply interested in something that was more appealing than racing home to face whatever troubles Rimrock, that was to say, Lear Holbrook, was experiencing. That which, or rather who, took precedence over Holbrook's orders was, namely, one Fanny Morris, featured singer and dancer, at the finest saloon in Laramie. She was also a companion of erstwhile nocturnal episodes in Roscoe Warren's life.

He stretched out upon the bed, his tousled mop of hair once again upon the pillows. To his nostrils came the faint aroma of Fanny's perfume, recalling the excitement of her nearness to him, and the intoxicating sweetness of her moist lips. He read the telegram again and, lowering it, gazed at the ceiling, balancing the feel of Fanny in his arms against the 150 miles of bouncing, jostling stagecoach trip to Rimrock.

His big fist slowly crumpled the telegram

into a wad and tossed it into the furthest corner of the room. He raised his watch from the stand beside the bed and glanced at the time. Merely 7.30. Fanny would not be ready for breakfast before ten. He lay back and closed his eyes. Lear Holbrook, and whatever his problems might be, would just have to wait another day, perhaps more than that, according to what kind of mood Fanny remained in. In fact, he would simply leave Laramie when he got good and ready. With that in mind, he blew a gust of air, turned over a couple of time in bed and drifted off again into sleep.

While the sheriff was squiring his old friend, Fanny Morris, in and out of the fleshpots of Laramie during her hours of leisure from her job at the saloon, Lear Holbrook was experiencing the most embarrassing time of his life.

As Matt directed Rainey and Holbrook from the saloon, he was met at the door by Al Rooney.

'Da' ya need an extra hand here, Matt?' asked Rooney, his cool eyes taking in the red, furious expression of Holbrook and the icy fury clouding the features of Holbrook's gunman.

'Well, you might kinda keep watch, mosey along with us over to the bank,' said Matt.

'Gonna make a deposit or a withdraw?' asked Al, laconically, falling in step with his boss and friend.

'Kinda like a withdraw,' said Matt wryly. 'You might as well come along. Our friends here don't like what I proposed.'

'They ain't likely to like anything they don't propose,' said Al, drily.

The four entered the bank. Al posted himself at the door, and Matt nudged the gunman and his boss up to a teller's window, the shotgun nakedly prominent to the view of anyone watching.

'Yes, sir, Marshal,' said Sam Withers, the middle-aged teller, 'just what can I do for you and these gentlemen?' His eyes then caught sight of the shotgun and the furious scowl on Holbrook's face. 'And, for you ... ah, Mr Holbrook...' he stammered.

'Mr Holbrook wants to make a withdrawal from his account,' Matt said. 'A rather substantial withdrawal.'

'No I don't!' yelled Holbrook. 'I won't write no check. This is plain bank-robbery!'

'Let me see,' said Matt, frowning. 'There's eighteen businessmen in this town. You've been milking them for two dollars extra a week for nearly a year. And just last month you upped it to five dollars. That was near all some of them cleared in a week. So ... to be fair about it, let's say you give back five dollars a week to each man for the amount you blackmailed them out of for a year. That could come to...' he squinted and figured in his head.

'Four thousand six hundred eighty dollars,' blurted the teller, 'or ninety dollars a man.' Then his hand went to his mouth. 'Oh hell ... I'm sorry, Mr Holbrook, I just didn't think!'

'Shut up, you fool! You ain't got nothin' to think with!' screamed Holbrook.

'By golly, Sam,' said Matt with a wry grin, 'you're exactly right. Just call it an even five thousand. Now, fill out a receipt so Mr Holbrook can sign it, and then count out the money in small bills.'

'I won't sign it!' Holbrook growled. The big hammers of the old shotgun made a loud *clicking* sound in the room. Holbrook paled, seized the pen and scribbled his name hurriedly in a nearly unreadable scrawl. At last, seeing that the circumstances were not those of one normally making a withdrawal, the teller disappeared into the vault. After a considerable time he returned

133

with both hands full of bills. He stacked them before Holbrook and hurriedly counted, finally pushing the piles over to the saloon-owner.

'Is ... is that all, Mr Holbrook? Can I do–'

'You've done enough!' Holbrook snarled, stuffing the money into the pockets of his jacket and pants. He whirled on Matt, bumped into the shotgun and hurriedly backed away.

'Is that all? Are you satisfied?' he asked, almost spitting in his fury.

'Nope.' Matt motioned them to the door. 'You gotta pay back the ones you *protected* with all this money,' he said.

'Well, just round them up and have them come to my office. I'll give them their money. But,' he shook a fist in Matt's face, 'you ain't heard the last of this.'

Al joined them at the door of the bank. Lance Rainey glared at him and then moved up beside his boss. Matt shook his head.

'You just don't get the picture, do you. Holbrook, you are through as boss of this town. You have your saloon and that is all. You find someone to run it for you and then retire to your ranch and be a rancher again. This town is no longer your plaything.'

Al Rooney walked behind the trio of Matt,

Holbrook and Rainey, his eyes sweeping the street, watching alleyways and glancing keenly at rooftops. Holbrook had men helping him keep Rimrock citizens in line. Not all of them would lie down and play dead over a couple of setbacks.

Townspeople grouped here and there as the word got out that Holbrook was paying back his 'protection' gain, under the menacing bores of Curtis's shotgun. The livery owner, the competing saloonkeeper, the barber – these received their money with bewildered looks until Matt explained that Holbrook had had a change of heart and was no longer running the town. The money was received with grimaces, grins and long faces, but none was refused.

Rooney's quick eyes caught a glimpse of a man easing out of the alley alongside the hotel. The man leveled a rifle at Matt.

Al's hand was a blur of motion, up and down, and the old sixgun roared. Matt jammed the shotgun into Holbrook's ribs and stopped him where he stood. Rainey whirled, his slim hand slapping his empty hip automatically and he cursed in frustration as he remembered he was unarmed.

The man beside the hotel reared back and screamed, the rifle discharging into the dirt before him, as Al's second shot drilled him just above the belt buckle, the .45 slug tearing his insides to rags. He twitched momentarily, sighed and was still.

'Matt, to your right!' yelled Al. Matt shoved Holbrook aside and whipped about, as a sixgun roared from the porch of Holbrook's own establishment. The shot whined by Matt's ear and the man was earing back his pistol to fire again, when Matt's shotgun boomed. The man was raised from his feet by the blast of the slugs from the .10 gauge shotgun, his chest torn apart. He slammed against the side of building and slid down, a smear of blood marking his descent against the boards.

Holbrook acted as though to run and Matt rammed the shotgun into his ribs again.

'Holbrook, you are losing men left and right,' Matt gritted. 'You ain't got many left. I have four in jail, just killed two, killed two in the basin and altogether put several others out of action. Now, when are you gonna wake up that you've shot your wad?'

Holbrook looked at him, his face sagging.

'Come on into my place,' he said, his voice no longer belligerent. 'Let's talk.'

Matt turned to Al. 'Go round up the

mayor, Silas Henry and a few more of the town council,' he said. 'Bring them to Holbrook's office. We'll get some things settled once and for all.'

Settled in the office, Matt motioned to the swamper.

'I know that you ain't the barkeep, but how about finding some of your boss's best whiskey and some glasses and bringing 'em in here. Holbrook is gonna have a meeting with the important people of Rimrock.'

The old swamper grinned toothlessly and scurried behind the bar.

'Sure will, Mr Curtis, so long as I get a little nip fer my trouble.'

'You've got your nip and out of the best bottle,' Matt observed drily.

Jake Forrest, the owner of the other saloon, and Tom Clogg, owner of the General Mercantile, came into the saloon, followed by Al Rooney. They all filed into the office, lining up along the walls. Al Rooney stood against the wall, just inside the door.

'Mr Holbrook has made rounds and returned a year's "protective" collection to every businessman in Rimrock, as you know,' Matt opened the meeting. 'He has decided to go back to ranchin' and leave his bar in the capable hands of some trusted individual.'

'How about all his rowdies who have roughed-up the town since he came here, and done his dirty work for him?' asked Silas Henry.

'Anyone he has appointed on his own, is no longer legal. The town council will appoint a marshal, elect a sheriff, select men and any other officials needed to run the town. Mr Holbrook has volunteered to step out of the picture. The rowdies you mentioned will leave town with him.'

Holbrook sneered. 'Volunteered with a ten-gauge shotgun at my back. And your outlaws killed my men when they were just protecting my holdings.'

Matt grinned. 'It won't wash, Holbrook. Everyone knows you tried to steal my hosses, and that you ain't filed any claim on the basin. Now, gentlemen, what are your wishes? Does Mr Holbrook remain a businessman in Rimrock, or is he out and you, the town council, take charge?'

'That's no problem,' growled the mayor. Mose Guthrie was a man who had grown up along the frontier trails of the West. He had fought his fight in the Civil War, and was no coward. Age had slowed him down physically and he was no longer packing a sixgun to back up any arguments. He looked about him and the rest of the council nodded.

'Very well.' He looked at Holbrook. 'You will be out of Rimrock by noon tomorrow,' he said. 'Take your watchdog here with you and any other hangers-on you have left around here. Appoint someone to run your businesses. Silas Henry will see that your hotel is attended to rightly, and will bank your money. You come into town for supplies and banking business. And that is all. You aren't welcome in Rimrock nor are any of your men. The town council is in charge of this town, and this time we aim to make it stick.'

His keen old eyes squinted and glinted as he talked and Holbrook had no come-back. Matt Curtis's sudden brashness and the surprising evidence of his strength on the town, had broken his hold upon the community. Holbrook's sole comment was a curse and a biting: 'Don't worry, Old Man! I'll be back and all of you will regret this day for the rest of your lives.'

The council filed out of Holbrook's office, grinning now that they were out from under Holbrook's thumb and his cut-throat gang.

Others were solemn, some wondering if they had done the right thing. What would happen if Curtis were removed from the scene? Would they have the backbone to stand up for themselves?

Outside the bar, the mayor lingered as the other council members scattered to their places of business. Matt rolled a cigarette and matched it, drawing smoke deeply into his lungs. Al leaned against the side of the building and watched the street with sharp eyes.

'Well, it's done,' Guthrie muttered. 'Now, if we have the guts to hold it, we will be all right.' He looked sharply at Matt. 'What about the sheriff? He's due back soon. And he's one of Holbrook's appointees.'

Matt shrugged. 'No one can see over the next hill, Mayor. We'll face that when we have to.'

CHAPTER THIRTEEN

Matt left Rimrock in the hands of the mayor and town council and returned to the basin a few days following Holbrook's ejection. He was anxious to examine his herd of horses, and, with Al Rooney, he spent most of the day looking them over.

At noon, Bill Smith called him aside as they were preparing to survey the herd again.

'Boss, I ran into something in the back part of the basin that might be of interest to you. Thought maybe you'd like to ride out and take a look.'

Matt eyed him thoughtfully. Rooney had reported that Smith was pulling his weight in the work about the basin. He nodded.

'All right. Come with Al and me this afternoon, and we'll take a look at what you have found.'

It was mid-afternoon when Smith guided them into a more or less secluded cove at the far end of the basin. He rode up to a sink, and nodded at it.

'I pulled a filly out of here a couple of days

ago. I think there'd better be a fence put around it, or we'll have to ride out every day or so to keep the horses out of it.'

Matt dismounted, went over to the pit, reached out and dabbled his fingers in the black mess. He surveyed the sink and its contents thoughtfully, then nodded slowly.

'I think we've run onto one of the reasons Lear Holbrook wants this basin, come hell or high water,' he said. He rose, wiped his hands on a handful of bunch grass, then re-mounted and looked at Smith.

'We'll keep quiet about this, Bill. I've got an idea as to why the basin seems to be import-ant to Holbrook. In the meantime,' he turned to Al, 'get a couple of men out of town who would like a day's work for real money, and fence this off from the rest of the graze.'

Al nodded and the three rode away to an-other small herd of horses they had yet to inspect.

For the rest of the day Matt spent much time thinking of what they had found on *his* property. Eventually he came to a conclusion and expressed his thinking to his partner. Rooney listened and nodded.

Roscoe Warren bid his old friend and erst-while bed-companion a reluctant farewell and climbed on the stage that would eventually take him to Rimrock. Fanny Morris waved to him from her bedroom window in the Laramie Hotel and threw him a kiss. Roscoe was not naïve. He knew Fanny would have another 'good friend' before the day was over, one who would pay her well.

After a long, bumpy ride in the stage from Laramie to Rimrock, Warren stepped out and stood, dusting himself with his hat, looking over the town. All seemed quiet. People were going about their everyday business as usual. Silas Henry came from the livery down the street and called to him.

'You gonna want your hoss, Sheriff?'

Roscoe wondered about the question. It was as though the old man knew he was supposed to go to the ranch.

'Yeah, Silas, get my roan saddled. I'll be along in a jiffy.' He took his valise and bundle of possibles from the stage-driver, and carried them to the hotel veranda, depositing them against the wall. Deciding on a drink before going to the ranch, he went to the saloon.

The barkeep saw him come in, and set out a glass and a bottle of Roscoe's favorite drink. As the former sheriff came to the bar, he poured a glass and pushed it toward him.

'This one is on the house. Welcome back, Sher – Roscoe.'

Roscoe raised an eyebrow and then nodded. 'What's goin' on around here, Pete? Silas Henry is in a hurry to saddle my hoss for me. You almost called me sheriff and then changed it. Have I missed something?'

Pete hurriedly polished a spot on the bar before him. 'Roscoe, you'd better go on out to the ranch an' talk to Holbrook before you do anything at all. There's been a heap of changes made around here. And you're part of them.'

Roscoe stared into his drink, and then downed in with a rapid gulp. He motioned for another.

'Where's my deputy, Williams?'

'The town council fired him. He's around somewheres,' the barkeep answered, pouring the drink. 'That Matt Curtis feller come into town. He ran a herd of hosses into the basin that Holbrook claimed was his. One of his pards was killed in a shoot-out in the basin, an' Curtis come in here an' talked the town council into makin' him marshal. Then he took a double-barreled shotgun an' cleaned up the town.'

Roscoe grunted. 'You sayin' I ain't sheriff

no more?'

Pete shook his head. 'I ain't sayin'. I'm jist repeatin' what I heard an' saw happen. Holbrook appointed you sheriff. The council unappointed you. They've telegraphed the governor at Cheyenne fer a new sheriff to be appointed by him. Governor telegraphed back there'd be one here in a month. That's why I said you'd better have a talk with Mr Holbrook afore you done anything else.'

Roscoe sipped the second drink. 'Where can I find this new marshal, this Matt Curtis feller?'

Pete shrugged. 'I'd say either down at the marshal's office or over in the hotel. Hear tell he's actin' kinda sweet on Emmy Henry. Or maybe he's out at his hoss ranch in the basin.'

Roscoe finished his drink, nodded to Pete and walked from the saloon. He had left Rimrock in the hands of Holbrook and his marshal, and come back to find the political field upside down. He was no longer sheriff, Holbrook had gone and the town was back in the hands of the town council. According to Pete, the bartender, he was out of a job. He fingered the sheriff's badge in his vest pocket and, grimacing wryly, turned and strode toward the marshal's office. The thought came to him, that perhaps he should have remained in Fanny's arms, after all.

He opened the door, stepped into the office and stood before the scarred desk behind which he was accustomed to seeing Willie Williams, Holbrook's appointed marshal. Instead, he met the steely eyes of Al Rooney, who sat in the marshal's chair and eyed Roscoe Warren calmly.

'You the new marshal?' asked Roscoe, pushing his hat back and eyeing the worn sixgun on Al's right hip.

'Nope.'

'Then why are you sittin' there? Where's the marshal?'

'I'm sittin' here 'cause the marshal is outta town an' asked me to set here an' answer questions like you just asked,' Al said, straight-faced.

Roscoe looked at the cells. In one was Two-finger Buck and another couple of Holbrook's usual town peacekeepers. In the other was the foreman of the Running LH Ranch. Tip Wilson. Tip stretched out on his bunk, grinned wryly at Roscoe.

'Well, well,' he said sarcastically, 'look who's back.'

Al spoke up. 'Yeah, that's the question. Just who are you, mister, and why all the questions?'

Without speaking, the ex-sheriff removed the metal emblem of his former position in the county, and tossed it with a clatter upon the desk. It came to rest before Al, the word SHERIFF reflecting dully on the tarnished metal.

'I reckon I won't be needin' this no more,' Roscoe Warren said, a wry twist on his lips. 'But, if I know Holbrook, I'll be seein' you again.' He stared intently at Al Rooney. 'What did you say your name was?'

'Didn't say. You just come in here and started talkin',' Al said, leaning back in the chair.

Warren nodded. 'I've seen you somewhere. It'll come to me an' maybe we'll talk then.'

'Hey, Roscoe,' Two-finger Buck called from his cell. 'Ain't you gonna turn us loose? We ain't done nothin', nothin' real wrong.'

'How about me?' Tip Wilson asked from his cell. 'I ain't done nothin' wrong either. Just tried to steal a feller's hosses, is all.' He grinned and winked at Al.

Roscoe waved a hand at the cells.

'You're Holbrook's problem, not mine. I'm on my way out to the ranch. I'll give the boss your greetin's.'

He stared hard at Al once more, meeting the cool sheen of the steady eyes. He nodded and left the office.

'Rooney, by the way,' Tip Wilson called from his cell, 'just where is the marshal, anyway? I ain't seen him at all in a couple of days.'

'He's out on business, his business.' Al grinned at Tip. 'You'll see him when he gets back.'

Matt Curtis and Emmy Henry were in a light buggy, drawn by a high-stepping bay mare. Matt had rented the rig and mare after inviting Emmy to a picnic. To his delight, she had accepted eagerly. He had left Al Rooney in charge of the jail for the day.

The day was warm, the sky blue, with only a few tufts of cottony clouds floating from south to north, bringing with them a warm breeze. Matt wanted Emmy to see where he intended building his ranch and home. It was nearing noon when he carefully guided the mare across the creek in the basin and drew up before the old, tumbled-down cabin where he, Al and Smith, had camped many times.

Emmy looked at the cabin, at the setting and turned wise eyes to Matt.

'I have a feeling you wanted me to see this place for some personal, important reason,' she said softly.

He nodded, his eyes warm with feeling as he looked at her. Emmy was not a beautiful woman. Her mouth was a little too large, her cheekbones a little prominent, the chin a bit heavy for the features. The beauty was in her eyes and hair. Her eyes were a deep, warm brown and wide, with long, dark lashes. The hair was dark brown, with a tint of red, clean, soft and shining as she moved her head. To Matt Curtis, she was the most beautiful woman he had ever seen.

'I wanted you to see this place,' he murmured. 'I aim to build my home just above where the old cabin stands, beside those two live-oak trees. See the giant pines in the back? The wind sings through them the year long. And the creek has fish in it and I aim to dig a well beside the house. I wanted you to see where we are going to live–'

She made a sound and turned her face to him, a blush rising to her cheeks. 'Where *we* are going to live, did you say?'

He took her hands in his own big, tanned fingers.

'Emmy Henry, I'm asking you to be my wife. We'll have a horse ranch with animals people will come from far and near to buy. It will be a dream come true and I've found the woman I want to share it with.'

Tears gleamed on the edges of her lashes and a smile trembled on her lips. She drew his face down to her own and her lips pressed his, soft and sweet and opening with desire and growing passion.

'Yes, Matt Curtis! Yes! Yes! I'll be your wife! I've dreamed of this moment since the first time you walked into the restaurant.' They clung together for long moments and then parted. He lifted her from the buggy seat and holding her arm, walked with her around the site. The living-room would be there, the dining-room there, the kitchen and the bedroom...

'Go on,' she breathed, her eyes shining, her hands clasping his tightly. 'Where will the bedroom be?'

He laughed and swung her up into his arms, her own twined about his neck.

'*You* have the honor of deciding that, my darling! And place it well, for it will be well used.'

She ducked her head and sighed.

'Ah, yes. And in that room we will beget sons and daughters to fill a great house, Matthew Curtis! And here you will begin a heritage that will reach beyond our years!'

CHAPTER FOURTEEN

The day following the picnic with Emmy Henry, and after a long silent period at his desk in the marshal's office, Matt Curtis opened the cells of Two-finger Buck and his two companions and set them free.

'You have an hour to get yourselves out of town,' he told them quietly, his eyes steely and his expression stolid. 'I can't keep you from coming back, but when you do, you behave yourselves, or you'll be right back here and the next time I'll keep you here until the circuit judge comes through. And that's about every six months, unless called. An' I ain't the callin' kind.'

The two companions slipped out of the jail immediately, but Two-finger Buck leaned over the desk and leered at Matt.

'You an' me are gonna have it out one day, with jist fists, buddy. No shotguns er hand-guns allowed.'

Matt grinned at him. 'We'll see. I won't hold my breath until it happens.'

Buck grunted. He took his hat, envelope

of small articles held for him, his gun belt and sixgun, and left the office, with one last malevolent leer at Matt.

Matt leaned back in the chair and looked over at Tip Wilson, now the only occupant of Rimrock jail.

'I reckon you might as well go, too, Tip,' he said. 'What are your plans once you are free?'

Wilson rose from the bunk and walked to the bars, showing only a slight limp from the wound received in the raid on Matt's horses. He shook his head.

'I don't rightly know, Matt. I know Holbrook won't want me at the ranch. He made Roscoe Warren foreman when he got back from Laramie. So that took care of me.' He was thoughtful for a moment, and then shook his head again. 'I reckon I'll just drift. There oughta be a job somewhere for a top hand.'

Matt eyed him thoughtfully. 'You got yourself into trouble being loyal to a hoss-thief, Tip. Only at the time you thought you were just to run my boys and the horses out of the basin. Now you know that Holbrook, once he got hold of my herd, would have sold them and kept the money for himself. That is what a good cowman does, Tip. Be loyal to his spread. But if the job turns sour, then what?'

Tip shrugged. 'I wouldn't work for Holbrook now, knowin' what I do about him, for any amount of money. So I guess I'll just mosey on. That's is, if the law lets me go scot free.'

Matt carried the key of the cell in his hand. He unlocked the door and swung it open, stepped back and motioned for Tip to leave the cell. He went back to the desk and produced an envelope holding the man's small possessions, coins, bills, and wallet. His gun belt and sixgun hung on a peg behind the desk.

He handed the possessions to Tip, then paused and looked the man in the eyes.

'Tip, I think you are a good man. There's an opening for another hand in my spread, small as it is. The job will primarily be breaking horses to riding, before I sell them to the army or the ranches nearby. The job is yours if you want it. Forty dollars and found. You supply your own saddle and gear.' He paused again for a moment, then continued:

'You are a free man, Wilson. If you want the job it is yours.' Matt eyed him carefully.

Moving slowly, thoughtfully, Wilson

stored the small items in his pockets. Matt handed him his belt and gun, which he swung about his waist and buckled. Only then did he straighten and looked Matt squarely in the eyes.

'You're treating me like a man, like I've seldom been treated afore this. Matt ... Mr Curtis, I accept your offer. What's my first orders?'

Matt thrust out his hand. 'It's Matt, Tip. Shake my hand on it. You're my foreman, now. I want you to round up at least four men, good men, and take them out to the basin. There's three boys there that need some relief and, I imagine, some more grub.'

'I can probably find some boys who are lookin' for work,' Tip said as he shook hands with Matt, both feeling the manly grip of the other.

'I'm gonna build a bunkhouse there by the old cabin, and when that's finished, I'll bring out a couple of carpenters and have them start on a house.'

'You got a woman to live in that house yet?' asked Tip, with a grin, raising his eyebrows.

Matt kept a straight face.

'Now, you know that a handsome, clean-livin', Christian man like me won't have any trouble findin' a wife, once I have a house to put her in.'

Tip took his hat from the rack beside the door, touched the brim with a finger in salute to Matt.

'If you say so, boss, if you say so.' He left the office with only a slight limp in the leg where he had been wounded.

Peace seemed to spread its soft blanket over Rimrock. Holbrook and his thugs were gone. People went about their business relaxed and at ease. Once more individuals remained on the street corners and in front of the places of business to gossip and pass on information. The town council was in control and there was seldom any disturbance of the euphoria that surrounded the community.

Matt took the opportunity at this time to make a trip to the territorial capital at Cheyenne. There he made acquaintance with individuals from whom he sought certain information. Satisfied with their answers, he returned to Rimrock with a knowledge that would rock Holbrook if the occasion arose.

Some of the more experienced citizens deemed it only a lull before the storm;

believed that Holbrook would be back in all his fury and it would be worse than before. But as the weeks went by and such predictions failed to come to pass, the town relaxed and went back to the way it was before Holbrook had brought in his devastating presence months ago.

Taking advantage of the peace that came to the town, Matt approached the council and persuaded them to hire a deputy marshal who would be in charge while he was occupied at his horse ranch. The nephew of Tom Clogg, the mercantile owner, was offered the position and accepted. Roy Clogg seemed right for the job, being a tall, quiet man of about thirty, with a wife and two children. For a week he followed Matt in the routine of rounds, checking the places of business after hours, and stopping a few fights between rowdy cowpokes who had had one or two drinks too many.

The deputy marshal felt he could handle the job by himself, with the promise of the town council to step in and help if necessary. Matt felt free to leave Rimrock and return to the basin where oak- and pine-logs were being cut and dragged to the place where he was determined to build his house.

'I'll be out to check on you every week,'

Emmy promised, a loving look in her eyes. 'Just to make certain you are getting the kitchen where it should be.'

The weeks passed. The peacefulness seemed to have arrived to stay. Holbrook had never entered the town from the time he had been ordered to leave. Workers came in and purchased supplies.

Rumors were heard that he was building an army out on his ranch, and would one day descend upon Rimrock and the old regime would be in charge again. But as time passed, the rumors died and the citizens of Rimrock sighed with relief. Maybe Holbrook had learned the lesson that he could not run roughshod over people for long and get away with it unscathed.

Matt seldom thought of the man. He was busy with his ranch and with the building of the house. A rider appeared one afternoon with a letter. Matt read it with interest and then nodded.

'So that was it,' he murmured to himself.

Tip Wilson found five men to work the horse ranch along with the three already there, keeping the horses moved from pasture to pasture, cove to cove. Some of the men worked with Matt and the two carpenters he had hired to build the house, barns and bunkhouse. The bunkhouse and cook shack went up quickly. An elderly man wandered in one day, riding a mule that appeared as elderly as himself. He was a ranch cook, out of a job, and looking for some ranch needing his abilities. Matt hired him on the spot.

It was not long before smoke rose from the chimney of the cook shack and the men gathered in for their first 'inside' meal at the new horse ranch. The other buildings were going up quickly and soon they would direct all their energy to the house.

Al Rooney was unspokenly looked upon as Matt's *secundo*. Wherever Matt happened to be, Al was always nearby. Tip Wilson was ranch foreman, but Al Rooney was second only to Matt in running the ranch.

One evening, after the men had eaten and retired to the corrals to check their personal string, or were lolling about the bunkhouse, smoking, reading outdated magazines, and talking, Al sat near Matt on a log that had been hewn for the house ridgepole.

'What are you gonna call this place, this hoss ranch?' Al asked.

Matt was thoughtful. 'You know, I have never really thought about that at all. It never even entered my mind.' He smoked quietly and looked beyond the clearing to the blue ridge of the basin to the west. 'You got any ideas what it might be called?'

Al thought for a long minute. He shook his head.

'How about "Curtis's Hoss Ranch"? That ain't very fancy, but it says what it is.'

Matt grinned. 'It does that all right. Well, for now, that will be what it's called.' He cocked an eye at Al. 'Who knows? Emmy may have some fancy name in mind.'

Al nodded, his face serious. 'Yep. She just may have. Women have fancies that men folk cain't even match.'

So 'Curtis's Horse Ranch' was the name of the new ranch in Rimrock basin, at least for the time.

The town of Rimrock might have been feeling the sweet touch of peace. And the citizens might have felt at ease. But Lear Holbrook was feeling otherwise.

The main house at the LH ranch was big, boxlike, with no pretense of beauty about it. It sat in the center of a congregation of sheds, bunkhouse, cook shack, well house, toolshed and tack-shed. The large barn for the animal food and the stalls were several hundred feet away from the main house.

There was no rhyme or reason about where the buildings were placed. Even the two outhouses that had been built, one for the main house and one for the bunkhouse, seemed perched haphazardly in place, within reasonable reach of each building, but with no sheltering bushes or shrubs or trees about them. There was a large pine tree alongside the main house, and some aspen near the corral back of the barn. Other than these all growth had been cleared away after the layout of the buildings was planned.

The main house consisted of two bedrooms, a kitchen, a large room which might have been a dining-room in the planning, and across the front of the house ran one long room, in the center of which was a huge fieldstone fireplace. One end of the room held Holbrook's desk and chairs and two other chairs for visitors. Throughout the rest of the room were scattered a huge horsehide divan, and two or three heavy chairs with a stand by each which might hold a lamp for reading. There were no rugs. One lone grizzly-hide lay stretched before the fireplace, eyes and teeth gleaming when the light caught them.

Holbrook had cheated the previous owner

160

of his present ranch out of the spread and had him mysteriously disappear in the mountains when he protested. Fearful of the outcome, no one had ever challenged him to prove positive ownership of the ranch. Once settled in he had created his own brand, rebranded all cattle and horses with the Running LH and claimed grazing rights for miles in any direction. It was later that he had added the Rimrock basin to his claim.

Holbrook was angry. Deeply bitingly, frustratingly angry. That one man might enter *his* town and take it from him, turn the citizens against him, was seemingly impossible. Yet, it had happened. Cool-eyed Matt Curtis, with a double-barreled Greener ten-gauge shotgun, had been too much for his 'boys', mostly men running from the law.

Lance Rainey, Holbrook's bodyguard and gunslinger, had so far proved ineffective. He sat before Holbrook at the moment, his face blank, as the Running LH boss fumed and stormed.

'You call yourself a "shootist",' Holbrook said with a bite of sarcasm in his voice. 'You prance around with a glare in your eyes and when one man – *one man,* mind you, comes on the scene, and tears up everything we've done in the past two years, you never turned your hand!'

'Boss, he had the drop on us every time with that cannon!'

'You just set there and let him take the town away from us, is what happened – and the basin as well!' Holbrook yelled, cursing and slamming his fist down on the desktop. 'What in hell do you think I'm payin' you top-gun wages for, if you can't do your job? Huh?' He rose and, leaning over the desk, glared at Rainey and shook a thick finger in his face.

I want that man Curtis killed! You hear? Killed!'

'There's always that Al Rooney on hand protectin' his back,' hissed Rainey, barely containing his anger, his face strained with effort. 'Rooney is a shootist from a way back an' if I try for Curtis with him there, he'll get me, too.'

'You're paid to take chances!' Holbrook yelled, his face staining red with his rage. He slowly settled back into his chair and sighed deeply.

'I'm paid to protect you, not to get myself killed by goin' up agin Curtis an' Rooney at the same time,' Rainey whispered.

Holbrook leveled a cold, cutting glare at him.

'You get Curtis, somehow. I don't care how – backshoot him if necessary. Then Rooney is yours to play with. But I want Curtis out of the game, and soon!'

CHAPTER FIFTEEN

After hiring more workers from Rimrock, and pushing the two carpenters he had brought out from town, Matt Curtis saw the house completed the last week of September.

Autumn was splashing its varied colors over the basin, aspen-leaves were yellow and beige against the deep green of pine and cedar; oaks flaunted deep brown and purple against the blue background of the basin rim. In the distance the mountains showed white tips as snow touched them, attesting to the approach of winter. Near the house piñons and aspen framed the cove in dancing leaves of yellow and red, with the purple of sage lifting away across the center of the basin.

A warehouse in Rimrock held the furniture Matt and Emmy had picked and ordered through the catalogues at the general store. Basic pieces to begin with. She was looking forward to a trip to Laramie or Cheyenne to finish off furnishing the house for the future.

Emmy spent as many days as possible watching the house being erected. She walked with Matt through the unfinished rooms and strolled the area, sat beside the creek and dreamed of the life to come with the man she loved.

The day the house was completed, painted and ready for rugs and carpets, they spent hours in the rooms. Matt built a small fire in the fireplace in the living-room, and they watched as the smoke was drawn smoothly and true up the chimney.

'A good draft,' murmured Matt. 'Everything looks good,' he said, smiling down into her bright face. 'And you look best of all. I think I'll just kiss you and keep on until we are married.'

'Promises, promises,' she whispered, throwing her arms about his neck. 'Why not start right now?'

The peace and accord of Rimrock and the basin ended abruptly one morning when Matt decided to visit Roy Clogg and see how he was making out as deputy town marshal.

Sitting with Roy in the marshal's office he found that all was not peaceful. Or would not be for long. Two-finger Buck was in town.

Drunk and up to his usual meanness, he had all but destroyed the smaller saloon that had long been in competition with the one owned by Lear Holbrook. In a fight in the saloon he had broken the jaw of one cowboy who had been too drunk to know better than to challenge Two-finger Buck when he was on one of his rampages. He had kicked another in the crotch so that he would be bent double for days. Both were mending on cots in Doc Marcus's back room.

Roy Clogg and four other men had eventually managed to bring Two-finger down and he was now in jail. Before turning him loose, the deputy wanted to talk about it with the marshal.

Matt leaned against the office desk and looked through the bars at Two-finger Buck. He shook his head.

'The last thing I said to you, Two-finger, was for you to get out of Rimrock and not come back. Remember?'

Buck came to the door and grinned with a gap-toothed spread of thick lips.

'Yeah, but you ain't got no reason to keep me outta town. By the way, when are we gonna have the fracas you more or less promised me?'

Matt shrugged. 'I'm not in much of a

scrappin' mood. Why don't you just pay for the damages you caused to the saloon, and go pay Doc Marcus for what he had to do for those two rannies you clobbered, then get yourself back to the ranch.'

Matt unlocked the cell door and handed Two-finger Buck his envelope of personal belongings, his hat and his sixgun. Buck slung the gun about his waist and buckled it. He jammed all the articles from the envelope: pocket knife, loose coins, a lucky piece, in his pockets and strolled to the door.

'Be seein' you, Marshal,' he said with a leer.

'Go on home, Two-finger. You're too mean for Rimrock. It can't take you and your kind anymore.'

The hulking form of Buck paused in the doorway, then disappeared. Roy Clogg listened to his heavy footsteps on the boardwalk, echoing, disappearing into the constant sounds of the town.

'There goes trouble, Matt. I think we oughta put him in a wagon an' haul him out in the mountains somewhere an' dump him in the deepest coulee we can find. One where he'd never find his way out.'

Two-finger Buck was determined to fight

the marshal. Not with guns. He knew he was no match for the marshal, especially when Matt carried the Greener with him. But with fists, now that would be another story.

He saw his opportunity step from the hotel, and approach him down the boardwalk toward the general store. Emmy Henry was on her way to the mercantile to buy supplies for the restaurant.

A slow grin spread the ugly mouth of the huge man. He lumbered along the board-walk toward her. As he drew near, Emmy noticed him and slowed, moving to the far inside of the walk, to let him pass.

Two-finger Buck was having none of it. He moved in front of her and stopped. As she shifted across the boardwalk to step around him, he stepped over in front of her. She stopped and looked him directly in the face. She was suddenly afraid. This huge man had been around town ever since Lear Holbrook had taken over. But he had never bothered her, other than to flirt or leer at her suggestively.

'Please let me pass,' she said softly, her voice shaking slightly with her nervousness.

'Naw.' He shook his massive head. 'You've been hoity-toity with me ever since I come to Rimrock. I reckon it's time we got acquainted real good.'

She attempted to step by him and again he moved over in front of her, refusing to let her pass. He reached out, moved his hand to her shoulder and slid it down, touching the front of her dress. She drew back swiftly and slapped at him, her face reddening with embarrassment and anger.

He laughed and a big paw moved and intercepted the blow.

'I guess a big kiss right here in front of Gawd and ever'-body will be jist right,' he tittered and wiped his thick lips with the back of his free hand.

She struggled and said with a clear, ringing voice, 'Let go of me, you bully! I'd rather kiss a hog than you!' She twisted in his grasp. Two-finger Buck grinned and pulled her close, his free hand pawing at her heaving bosom.

For some reason Matt Curtis left his chair and stepped to the doorway. Then he heard the loud guffaw down the street and a woman's voice raised in anger. He stepped out onto the boardwalk just as Emmy jerked her hand loose from Buck's grasp and slapped him resoundingly on his ugly mouth.

'Why … you little…' His words reached

Matt's ears. The marshal stepped into the street and walked toward the struggling couple as Buck grabbed Emmy's arm and pushed her against the side of the building in front of which they had met.

'Why don't you pick on someone nearer your size?' Matt's voice reached from the street where he paused close by to them.

Two-finger Buck released Emmy and turned slowly, facing Matt with a wide grin on his face.

'Waal, now,' he rumbled. 'I thought that would bring you outta yer den. Are you finally gonna fight me?'

'However you want it, Buck. Guns, clubs, fists – you name it, you got it.'

'Naw. I don't have to use anything but my fists, Marshal. Them's all I've ever needed. Hits all I'll need fer you.' As he spoke he unbuckled his gun belt and let it slide to his feet. He stepped off the boardwalk into the street, facing Matt.

Matt nodded, unbuckled his own belt and laid it on the walk. He wore a white shirt and slowly rolled up the sleeves, baring and freeing his muscular forearms. Two-finger Buck stood waiting, grinning. Then he spat into the dust and, quickly for one so large, launched a whistling blow at Matt's head.

The marshal dodged and as the big man twisted past him, he gathered all his strength and sank his fist into Buck's kidney area. Two-finger grunted and staggered. He turned and lumbered toward Matt again, his face twisted in pain and anger. This was supposed to be an easy match. The marshal simply could not hurt him nor stand up to him like this.

Two LH men had come into town with Buck and had been waiting to see if he would be released from jail. Now they came out of the saloon and, seeing the fight, approached at a fast walk.

Roy Clogg came from the mercantile and seeing the two men advancing as though to take part in the fracas, called to them.

'You two men stay right where you are. Let them fight it out. It's been comin' on a long time.'

The two men stopped and faced him. Seeing the sixgun in his hand, they demurred and stepped back upon the walk and leaned against the mercantile porch posts.

'The marshal ain't gotta chance, no ways,' one of them commented.

Others observing the fight might well have been of the same opinion. Buck connected with a whirling right fist, which caught Matt in the chest. It hurt, bending bones, but the worst was the power of the blow, sweeping him back and off his feet. He tumbled and rolled in the dust of the street. Ribs gave painfully and he rolled again, this time into Buck's advance. Catching his legs, he jerked him down. The two men rose and lurched at each other again, both winded and hurt from blows they had traded and received.

Emmy watched the fight, frightened as she saw the unknown strength of the huge man pitted against the slim, wiry, twisting form of her sweetheart. She knew he had recovered from the former beating he had taken, and that Buck had been the instigator of that fight, through the urging of Lear Holbrook.

Matt was tiring. He heard the gasping breath of his opponent and knew the big man was also tiring rapidly. Here was opposed slovenly living, too much beer, late nights, careless eating, against a younger body, well set up, very little drinking, and working long hours in the open air. Matt was in the better shape and his youth, cared-for health and strong muscles from hard work, were beginning to tell on the bigger man.

Two-finger Buck knew he had to finish the fight quickly or he would lose. For the first time in years, he became fearful he was going to be bested in a fistfight. He rushed Matt and managed to seize him with one long arm. He began to pound him with the other fist; hard, cruel blows to the body and the face of the smaller man came quickly and ruthlessly.

The two stood toe-to-toe and traded blows. Matt's hard fists sank into the soft belly of Buck and the big man gasped for breath. As he backed away, he shaped up to throw a roundhouse punch at Matt. Seeing the blow coming, Matt stepped inside the swing and struck with his right, putting all his strength into the blow. His fist flashed in to land with a resounding crunch against the point of Buck's jaw in front of his left ear.

Buck staggered. His eyes blurred and he turned aimlessly toward Matt, pawing the air with his huge, hamlike hands. Matt gathered his strength. He sank a left deep into the pit of Buck's belly, just above the belt buckle, then crouched and drove a right fist directly to the point of Buck's chin. There was a crack, like the sound of one plank slapping against another.

The big man walked backwards on wobbly heels. He hit the edge of the boardwalk and fell back across it, his huge body falling loosely, out of control. The boards clattered and dust sprang in the air as the body bounced. Two-finger Buck lay unconscious, knocked out by that last blow to the chin.

Matt stood, straddle-legged, his chest heaving with the effort to breathe. Blood seeped from a cut on his forehead. He staggered over to the mercantile porch, leaned against a post, then slid down to sit loosely, weak and trembling from the punishment he had taken to win the fight. Emmy cried out at the sight of his bleeding face and ran to him. She knelt and, taking the kerchief from around his neck, she tried to staunch the bleeding.

One of the LH men looked at the other and shook his head.

'I never thought I'd ever see that. Two-finger Buck beat to the ground with fists – not even a club ner a gun barrel used on him.'

The other man grunted.

'Let's get back to the ranch. I gotta tell Holbrook about this!'

CHAPTER SIXTEEN

Peace had indeed run its course and was slowly evaporating from Rimrock and the basin. The only person who knew that it was true was Lear Holbrook. He called in Roscoe Warren and motioned him into a chair in front of the desk behind which he sat.

'Roscoe, I want you to take a crew and take out that horse ranch in the basin. I hear they've built a house, barns, bunkhouses and corrals. I want them all destroyed, and Matt Curtis along with them.'

'About the only way that can be done, boss,' Roscoe drawled, 'is to burn 'em out. An' to do that means we gotta kill off the whole bunch of 'em before we can fire the place.'

'Whatever has to be done, do it.' Holbrook waved a hand. 'In the meantime, while you're doing that, I'll take the town back over and we're in business again.'

Roscoe raised an eyebrow at Holbrook.

'Tell me, Boss, jist what is it about that

basin that makes it so important to you?'

'Right now, that ain't none of your business, Roscoe. You just do what I tell you to do, and when the time is ripe, you'll know all about it. Now, get busy on what I told you to do.'

As the two men in Rimrock walked to their horses prior to mounting and taking the message of Two-finger Buck's beating to their boss, Matt Curtis, sitting on the edge of the mercantile porch, called to them.

'Where are you two going?'

The men turned and looked at him. One of them sauntered closer to him and peered at Emmy, who was wiping his battered face with a wet cloth given her by Tom Clogg, owner of the store.

'In the shape you're in, I reckon you cain't make it your business where we go, Mister Deputy.'

Roy Clogg, the deputy marshal, stood to one side of where Emmy was working on Matt.

'An' I reckon you'd better answer the marshal, or I'll just march both of you off to the hoosegow for a day or two.'

The other cowboy came over, leading the horses.

'Deputy, we are goin' to the ranch to report to Mr Holbrook about you beatin' poor ol' Buck thar half to death.' He grinned as he said it.

Matt nodded towards the now stirring body of the big man.

'Get him on his hoss an' take him to the ranch. Keep him out of town. And tell Holbrook that the town's off limits to the LH crews if he can't keep his men under control.'

The man nodded grimly. With his companion he lifted Buck into the saddle of his horse and leading by the reins, trotted out of town, dust rising and settling from the horse's hoofs.

Matt rose and leaned against the post nearest him, shrugging his shoulders and wincing at the pain of the bruises left by Buck's sledgehammer blows.

'Are you all right, Matt?' Emmy looked at him worriedly, her eyes taking in his battered features.

He nodded, grimacing as he did so.

'Nothing seems broken. Just rolled over by an elephant.' He grinned wryly. He picked up his gun and belt and swung them about his hips, buckling it in place. 'I'll go over to my room an' wash up a bit,' he grunted. 'I'll see you at dinner-time.'

Roscoe Warren clumped into Holbrook's ranch office and slouched into a chair. He laid his hat on the floor beside the chair and looked at his boss.

'I just figured out the time to hit that hoss ranch an' burn it to the ground. There won't be more than a couple of men around at the time an' they won't give us much trouble. Either they'll take to the hills, or we'll blast them to kingdom come.'

Holbrook leaned back from the ledger he was working on and looked at his foreman. When Roscoe had shown up, no longer sheriff, and Lear learned that Tip Wilson had gone over to work for the horse ranch, Holbrook had appointed Warren foreman of the LH ranch.

'What's your scheme?' he asked, reaching and taking his smoldering cigar from the ash tray beside him.

'There's a shindig, a dance, in town next Saturday night. It's a seasonal thing, I think, just before Thanksgiving. Everyone in the county will be there.'

'And you and the boys will visit Curtis's place and put it to the torch while everyone is in town, is that it?'

Warren nodded. 'Yep, that's it, boss. They won't leave but a couple of fellers back to watch the place. They won't be no trouble. By the time the dancin's done in town, the buildin's at Curtis's hoss ranch will be just piles of ashes.'

Holbrook was silent for a long moment, drawing on his cigar and letting the smoke slowly trickle from his lips. Then he nodded.

'Not bad, Roscoe, not bad. Do it. Make sure every stick of that house, barns, sheds, everything standing, is burned to the ground.'

Roscoe nodded. He rose and left the room, leaving Holbrook to his thoughts. Here was a chance, at long last, for him to take over the town again. He would see that sometime soon, following the burning of Curtis's place, Lance Rainey would meet Curtis and gun him down. That would leave them clear to be in charge of the town, and the surrounding territory as well.

Holbrook leaned back in his chair and savored his smoke, clasping his arms about his head. This, and what he could do with the basin, with Curtis gone, would put him on top again. His mind played again with the day he'd discovered that sink-hole on the back mesa of the basin.

Al Rooney looked wryly at Matt's bruised face and shook his head.

'It sure is gettin' dangerous for me to let you go anywheres by yourself, boss. What kind of wildcat did you meet up with this time? Or did Miss Emmy catch you flirtin' with the parson's wife?'

Matt grinned and shrugged. He had returned to the basin the day following his fight with Buck. His ribs were sore, his knuckles skinned and he sported an eye that competed with the purple sage for color.

'I'd probably have come out worse, if it had been like you said,' Matt commented. Sitting on the edge of the porch of the new house, he looked over the meandering creek at the foot of the slope as he related to Al his contest with Two-finger Buck.

Al had remained at the ranch, to oversee some final work on the corrals, and to check with the wranglers working with the horses further over toward the mountain rim of the basin. They were in the process of culling the herd.

The poorest of the lot would be sold for whatever could be gotten for them. The best mares and studs would be held back for breeding purposes. The remainder of the herd was to be sold in bulk to the army or to ranches in the area needing mounts for the fall round-up and general work on the spread.

'Ah hear thar's to be a shindig in town come Saturday night,' Al said. He sat, his lean body relaxed, but his pale eyes swept the basin across the creek, watching the shadows change on the slopes leading the mesa, never still, seeing everything before him.

'Yeah. They call it the "fall festival" or something like that. I guess they want to get it over with before the snows set in.'

'From the looks of the mountains there, they'd better get it done,' Al said, nodding to the peaks above the mesa. The white caps of the peaks were creeping lower by the day. 'We'll be gettin' our first snows afore long.'

'You plan on takin' us to the dance?' he asked Matt, after a pause while both rolled cigarettes and drew in the first long breaths.

'I reckon so,' Matt murmured. 'Emmy has a new dress for it, and if I don't squire her to the dance, she just might look somewhere else for someone to prance with her and show it off.'

Al grinned. 'Then I guess we'll be goin' to the dance,' he said. His face settled into grim lines, far from the gentleness of their former conversation. With everyone at the dance, the ranch would be unguarded. He was not one to believe that Holbrook would not attempt some kind of retaliation against Matt and the basin. And such a thing as the dance, with the entire community there ... his thoughts ran long and grim at the thought of what might happen to the ranch, left unguarded.

The stage from Laramie rolled into Rimrock and drew up before the hotel. Ned Baker the driver, clambered down and called to the passengers inside the stage.

'This is Rimrock, folks. There's a change of hosses here and a stay of about forty minutes. The hotel thar has a dinin'-room an' other needful places of necessity.'

As he went to the boot of the stage in the back and unlashed several pieces of luggage, the stage emptied. One man came around the end of the stage and waited for his valise and a long leather object, obviously a rifle in a sheath. He nodded to the driver, then turned and entered the hotel lobby.

He did not appear as a big man, in spite of his six feet in height and wide shoulders. He had the slim hips of a horseman and the tanned face of one living and working in the elements of this country. His features were slim, bronzed, with eyes wide-set and green. The nose was long and full, and the mouth wide and generous, one that could laugh with rich humor or thin down to a quick run of temper. The left hand, holding the valise, was slim-fingered and strong; the right hung to his side, fingertips brushing the butt of a holstered sixgun.

He was dressed in the garb of a range man, solid jacket, dark sturdy pants and boots, which, while dusty, showed richness of leather. He walked to the lobby desk and nodded to the clerk.

'I'd like a room, if one is available,' he said, his voice quiet and firm.

'We have rooms, mister. Just sign the book here and I'll get your key. Bathhouse is in the back of the barbershop down the street and we have our own dining-room.'

The man nodded his thanks, took the pen from the clerk and signed his name. He picked up his valise and mounted the stairs, looking at the number of the room key.

The clerk turned the book around to read the name the stranger had written. The name 'Todd Bonner' was inscribed boldly and legibly.

CHAPTER SEVENTEEN

Matt leaned on the corral gate, watching a rider work on a mare he was breaking in for Emmy. The man knew what he was doing, easy with the animal, taking the time necessary to make her into a gentle riding mare for his boss's sweetheart.

Hearing a horse approaching, Matt turned and watched as the rider came up and raised a hand in greeting.

'Howdy,' the man said. 'I'm looking for Marshal Curtis.'

'You've found him,' Matt said with a scanning glance at the man. Friendly face, greenest eyes he had ever seen in a man, sixgun on right hip. 'I'm Curtis. What can I do for you?'

'I'm Todd Bonner, Marshal. I'd like a word with you if you have the time.'

Matt nodded. The Western courtesy of remaining mounted until invited to light down was being observed.

'Step down, Mr Bonner. I was just going to the cook shack for a cup of java. Join me?'

187

Bonner stepped down and hitched the reins to a corral post.

'That sounds just right, Marshal. Lead the way.'

Over coffee and a plate of day old 'bear signs' that Cookie had placed before them, the two men became acquainted. Talk was about the horse ranch and the little town of Rimrock that Bonner had just come through. He had taken a room at the hotel, but his intentions were to find the town marshal and ask him some questions.

'Matt,' Bonner eyed him thoughtfully, 'keep what I am going to tell you now under your hat. I'm a deputy United States marshal. I had myself appointed so I could cross territorial lines, and find a man and take him back to the Dakotas to stand trial for murder. I got word he was in this area and had an idea you just might know the man and where I might locate him.'

Matt sipped his coffee and listened.

'Where in the Dakotas?' he asked.

'A little town called Sundance, on the Sundance Creek. I have a ranch about five miles out of the town, the Bar T-and-N. It used to be the Bar F spread before – before the woman I married inherited it.' He grinned wryly.

Matt shrugged. 'One never knows how those things happen,' he commented. He called the old cook for more coffee and when it was poured and they were alone again, he said:

'How can I help you, Bonner?'

'About two years ago a fellow by the name of Lear Holbrook landed in Sundance and took over the town. Before anyone knew what was happening, he had his roughnecks in place and was in control of the town, with his own law, judge, his 'protectors', who protected the businessmen by extracting a weekly fee. Eventually the citizens, encouraged by a man named Wade Manning, bucked Holbrook's gang and drove them out. Holbrook followed and deliberately shot Manning in the back, killing him instantly. He left a wife and boy, with no man to look after them. Holbrook ran and disappeared. It has taken this long for him to surface and for word of him drift back to Sundance.'

'Then you want him for murdering this man Manning?' asked Matt. 'Did you have yourself appointed US marshal, just for this job?'

Bonner nodded, his face grim.

'Wade Manning was my friend. At Shiloh, during the war, he was my captain. He saved my life more than once. I owe it to him, and to his wife and son, to see Holbrook in prison for what he did.'

Matt nodded. 'I see. Well, your search is ended. Lear Holbrook came into Rimrock two years ago, and pulled the same thing here he did at Sundance. Only here the people put up with it longer, apparently not wanting to face the fight needed to get him out.'

'How did they get him loose of the town?' asked Bonner.

Matt grimaced wryly. 'Well, he killed a pard of mine, so I took a double-barreled Greener shotgun and kinda persuaded him to leave.'

Bonner nodded seriously. 'I reckon a Greener in the hands of someone willing to use it would persuade just about anyone who wanted to keep his hide so it would hold water.' He was silent a moment and then asked:

'Where would I find Holbrook?'

'If you can get close to him, he has a ranch about five miles out of Rimrock. It's called the Running LH, with the brand of LH. It fits the man and his habit of stirring up trouble and then hightailing it, I reckon. But I warn you, Todd, he has gathered about him a bunch of hardcases. And he has a guard dog named Lance Rainey, who is reputed to be a cold-blooded killer.'

'He didn't seem to stop you from running Holbrook out of Rimrock,' Bonner said drily.

Matt shrugged. 'I got the drop of them and with that shotgun grinning at them every step of the way, Holbrook kept his gunnie on rein.'

Bonner stretched and rose. 'Guess I'll be moseying back into town,' he said. 'Thanks for the information. I'll figure out a way to get at Holbrook. He can't be under Rainey's eye all the time.'

As they left the cook shack, Al Rooney pulled up to the hitch rail and dismounted. He started toward the cook shack and seeing Matt and Bonner, stopped where he was, eyeing Bonner closely.

'Bonner, this is my foreman, Al Rooney. Al, meet Federal Marshal Todd Bonner.'

Al's pale eyes remained steady as he reached out a browned hand and clasped that of the federal marshal.

'Al Rooney,' said Bonner, thoughtfully. 'I guess Holbrook isn't the only one in these parts who has a fastgun on pay. I seem to have heard of you, Al.'

Al nodded coolly. 'Word gets around, Marshal, true or otherwise,' he murmured, his eyes steady on the lawman's face.

Matt glanced at Bonner. 'Al has been with me for a long time, Todd. Whatever is past, is past, and he is my right hand and partner in this hoss enterprise. I think of him as you did the man Holbrook had murdered. He's my friend.'

'I know you rode with Quantrill, Rooney. That gave you a bad name. But bad names can be lived down and I take Matt's word that you've done that.'

Rooney looked at him, his eyes narrow and piercing. His voice was thin and strained and hard and it was evident his next words came from him with effort.

'I said this only once, to Matt here, a long time ago. I'll say it to you and your ears only. I rode away from Quantrill's bunch when I heard what he planned for Lawrence, Kansas. I never looked back.' He held Bonner's gaze, his eyes never wavering. His body was relaxed, his arms across his chest.

Bonner nodded. 'You didn't even have to say that, Rooney. Your word is as good as your bond, so far as I am concerned.' He held out his hand to Rooney. The older man held his gaze for a long moment and then took his hand in a hard clasp. No more words were spoken. None was needed. Their handclasp had sealed their trust each in the other.

'Just to clear the air,' Al drawled, 'I've heered of you, too. Jist a little, something about bein' purty slick with a gun, yerself.'

Bonner smiled wryly, and repeated Al's former comment.

'Like you said, Al. Word gets around, true or otherwise.' Matt chuckled and a crooked grin crossed Rooney's lips.

The dance was on Saturday night. Bill Smith came up to Matt just before the boss was leaving the ranch.

'I think I'll just stick around the camp, Matt. I ain't much of a dancer.'

Matt looked at him and then shrugged.

'That's up to you, Bill. You may be needed here, who knows.'

When Matt left with the others who were going to the dance, Tip Wilson remained behind.

'I've got a little feeling,' he told Al, 'that we might have some visitors tonight. It would be just the time for Holbrook to try something against Matt and the basin.'

Al looked at him and nodded slightly.

193

'Them's my thinkin' too.' He looked at Bill Smith as Tip left to take up a place of concealment from where he could watch the entrance to the basin.

'Why did you stay behind, Bill?' He eyed the younger man quietly, a tilt of a smile on his lips. Smith shrugged.

'Like I said, I ain't much fer dancin'.'

'When I was young like you, a dance was the finest thing ever comin' to town. To see them pretty gals, and to swing 'em, was somethin' I purely enjoyed.'

Smith was silent a moment and then nodded.

'It's fine, all right. An' I've swung a few of them gals. But I have an eye on a little piece of land down in Texas, around the Red River area. I'm tryin' to save up a little cash. If it works out, I'll be workin' fer myself.'

Al nodded. 'Sounds good to me.'

Back of Tom Clogg's mercantile store was a flat area upon which, from time to time, a platform was laid, with benches alongside for the 'wallflowers'. Being outside while the weather was good, avoided the heat generated by being within walls, with many bodies in action. The town fathers paid for the dance platform, hired the musicians, and realized far more across the counters from goods purchased than was spent on the creation of a dance platform. It was good business for all.

Matt arrived at the Henry apartment to find Emmy ready and waiting, her face alight with anticipation. He handed her a small bouquet which she immediately placed in a vase on a small stand near the door.

'Your escort for the evening is both handsome and gallant,' her father told her as he went to the door with them. 'You have a good time now, hear?'

'Aren't you coming, Daddy?' Emmy asked.

'Oh, sure. I'll be along after awhile. Dancing is more for you youngsters than us oldsters.'

'Well, anyway, don't be too late,' she said, rising and kissing his cheek. 'Remember, I save one waltz for you.'

'I might just be able to handle a slow one like that,' Silas said with a smile. 'Now, get on with you, and have fun.'

The crowd was gathering when Matt and Emmy arrived at the dance floor. Musicians, placed on a platform in one corner, were scraping and tuning, getting ready for the first round.

'Howdy, Marshal, Miss Emmy.' Roy Clogg stood at a table to one side of the floor. Upon it were gun belts, tagged and laid aside for the evening. No weapons were worn on the dance floor.

'Evening, Roy.' Matt returned his greeting. He unbuckled his weapon and placed it on the table. Emmy spoke to Roy and then, holding Matt's arm, entered the dance area.

She felt Matt stiffen. She turned. Looking across the floor as a couple moved away from them, she saw Lear Holbrook and Lance Rainey standing beside the table of refreshments, each with a drink in his hand.

She felt Matt move as if to draw away from her, but she clutched his arm.

'Let it go, Matt, please. For this one evening, let it go. Let everyone have a good time, with no trouble.'

'I told him to stay out of Rimrock, and I meant it,' Matt gritted, his face darkening in anger. His wrath was fired higher when Holbrook smiled, nodded and raised his glass to him in a mocking salute. The thin lips of Rainey moved in a smirk.

'This is different,' she pleaded. 'Please, let it go. For tonight, ignore him.'

Matt looked at her and saw the earnestness of her face, the pleading in her eyes, moisture gathering around the edges. He softened and she felt him relax.

He nodded stiffly and briefly.

'They are trying my patience. Besides, there's not much they can do out in the open with the whole county watching.'

The musicians struck up a slow dance and Emmy moved into his arms. With the woman he loved against him, the softness of her body, and her smile for him alone, he turned aside the problems of the moment and gave himself over to the enjoyment of his dance with her in his arms.

After two or three pieces of slow dancing, the caller for the dance rose and got their attention.

'Now you've all got the romance out of your systems, let's get some action out there on the floor. The next piece is a rousin' square dance. So, grab your pardners and form your squares and here we go!'

The musicians struck up one of the old square-dance tunes, 'Turkey in the Straw', and the caller began to shout the movements. In an instant the floor was whirling with the action of the dance. Dresses flounced, boot-heels scraped and feet pounded out the rhythm.

Lear Holbrook and Lance Rainey had moved from the refreshment table to stand just off the edge of the platform. Night had fallen. Beyond the light of the lanterns placed on poles about the dance platform, it was dark. The darkness was disturbed here and there by groups of men gathered to talk and visit, rather than dance. Others sought certain jugs hidden out in buckboards and saddlebags for more serious refreshment.

'I don't see any of the Curtis bunch, other than the boss dancing with the storekeeper's girl,' Holbrook mused to Rainey. 'Circulate around and see if there's any more of his hoss wranglers in town.'

Rainey disappeared silently into the darkness. Holbrook edged back until he was in the shadows beyond the nearest lantern. He was suddenly uneasy. There should have been more of Curtis's men out there on the dance floor, enjoying themselves, swinging the girls.

Several minutes passed and as silently as he had slipped away, Lance Rainey was back at Holbrook's side.

'I didn't see many of Curtis's men,' he hissed in Holbrook's ear. 'Well, there's two at least and the boss himself there dancin'. They ain't got a big crew, so it looks like they split in half and half, maybe drawed straws, or something – anyway, that's all I could see.'

'Then somehow they've found out Roscoe is going to jump the basin tonight,' Holbrook said, cursing. 'How in hell did they find out? Someone must have gotten drunk and leaked the plan.'

He stiffened. His eyes narrowed and he stepped quickly back into darker shadows.

'Do you see who just stepped onto the dance floor?' He nodded toward the front of the area.

Todd Bonner left his gun at the table with the deputy town marshal, and stepped up to the dance platform, looking about him.

'Something's gone wrong,' Holbrook said savagely under his breath. 'What is he doing here? Let's get back to the ranch.'

He and his human shadow slipped back away from the crowded dance floor and sought their horses. In a few minutes they had left the town at a gallop.

CHAPTER EIGHTEEN

The elements worked in Roscoe Warren's favor, or so he thought. The autumn moon was full, round and high. The silvery glow highlighted every aspect of the Curtis horse ranch buildings, corrals and surrounding area. He sat with twelve men about him on a small slope, a mile from the house.

'You see any activity around the place?' he asked one of the men at his side. The man squinted for a few minutes, surveying the scene before him. The buildings were dark. There were no lights shining from the windows of the house or the bunkhouse.

'There's a light in the cook shack,' he muttered. 'But whoever he left on guard would be there, drinking coffee and playing euchre, most likely.'

'A couple of men, I'd judge,' Warren answered. He stirred in the saddle. 'All right, men. Let's do it!' There was the squeak of leather as the men stirred, the sound of rifles being loosened in sheaths. 'Let's go,' called Warren, and the group moved out of the shadows, racing across a wide meadow toward the entrance to the basin. They splashed across the creek and up the slope to the buildings and whirled with thundering hoofs into the wide area between the main house and the barns.

Matt saw Lear Holbrook and his shadow, Rainey, slip away from the dance area. He was dancing a slow dance with Emmy and saw that Todd Bonner had stepped upon the floor. He moved with Emmy to the side and came up to Bonner.

'Holbrook just left,' he said to Bonner. 'If you'll take Emmy home when she is ready, I'll leave and see if I can beat them to the ranch.'

'Matt ... what's wrong?' Emmy asked, her voice suddenly tight with an unknown fear.

In a tense voice he told her his suspicions of the attack on the ranch. Bonner listened and then spoke.

'Emmy, I'll go with Matt. Your father just arrived. He will see you home when you are ready to go.'

She nodded. Suddenly she leaned up, and to the amusement of those close by, gave Matt a resounding kiss right on the mouth.

'You be careful, darling,' she whispered. 'I

have a lifetime to live with you and a lot of babies to have.' With that she left him and went to her father, quietly telling him what was taking place.

In a few minutes Todd Bonner and Matt were on their horses racing out of Rimrock toward Matt's ranch.

Roscoe Warren drew his horse to a skidding halt and twisted about, looking at the buildings. There were no lights, except from the cook shack. The yellow lamp-glow angled out of a narrow panel into the yard. Strange, thought Warren, that the door is open when it's chilly enough to keep it shut. This ain't summertime. But the thought flashed by and was forgotten.

The men swirled about him. He rose in his saddle and bellowed:

'Burn the place to the ground!' He aimed his horse at the porch of the main house, and waved some of the men with him. 'Go in and set fire to it!' he yelled. He drew his gun, fired at the cook shack and yelled again: 'Go get whoever's in there an' bring 'em out. Tie 'em up, an' burn it.'

As his gun fired, the *crack* of a rifle answered his shot and one of the men who had dismounted to enter the house, stumbled back, screamed and clutched his chest. A fusillade erupted from three different points, guns roared and somewhere a shotgun blasted its devastating scatter.

The LH men were caught from three different directions. Matt and Al Rooney had worked it out. Counting Al, the cook and one of the carpenters, along with Bill Smith, there were six men hidden in three different places: the house; the corrals, now empty and the animals all hidden in the back of the basin; and the sheds between the bunkhouse and the main house. Bales of hay had been spread about for protection and concealment.

As the rifle fired from the house, stopping the invasion of LH men, all guns from the other points began a sweeping fire where the LH men had scattered. The moon was at its highest, huge and round and bright. The area where the LH men milled about, seeking targets, was as light as day.

Roscoe Warren was appalled. It had not occurred to him that any man, given the opportunity to leave behind humdrum duties after long months of containment, and attend an evening of dancing and drinking, would not do so. But it was quickly obvious to him that he had led his crew into a well-planned and positioned trap.

Around him men were crying out, yelling in anger and surprise, firing at muzzle blasts only. The light in the cook shack had been doused and gunfire was erupting from the door and the window nearest where his men were caught.

Horses squealed and fell, men cursed and still the gunfire poured into them. Several men were down and more were wounded. Roscoe Warren made his decision. Let Lear Holbrook think of something else. This was a disaster.

'Break it off! Come on, men, let it be! Let's get out of here!' He whirled his horse and bulled his way through the milling, rearing, shouting mêlée, getting the attention of his crew. Forcing his way through, he guided his horse beyond the corrals and, raising his sixgun, fired three shots into the air.

Hearing his shouts and his three-shot signal to gather on him, six men broke away from the fight and gathered around him. Panting, cursing, two of them wounded, they whirled about Warren. He made quick count.

'There's seven of us. You mean that six of us got it back there?' he asked, astonishment in his voice.

'I know two are plumb dead, Roscoe. Hank Willow and Tack Bellows got it. The rest are hurt purty bad an' can't get on their hosses.'

Warren was silent a moment, then he sighed gustily.

'Well, we can't fight that bunch no more, hid the way they are. Maybe they'll let us pick up our dead and wounded. I'll see...' He broke off as two riders broke out of the tree line a mile away and came pounding toward the ranch.

'That isn't any of our crew, Roscoe,' one of the men yelled. 'It's more of the Curtis bunch.'

'Everyone holds steady,' Warren said. 'We'll see who they are and go from there.'

Matt Curtis and Todd Bonner drew their horses to a quick stop facing the LH crew spread across the trail. Matt, with a quick glance, saw that some of the men were wounded. He knew the fight was over.

'Who are you men and what are you doing on my spread at this time of night?' he asked, his voice cold and direct.

Warren answered. 'We're LH, and just got ourselves whopped real good by whoever's dug in back there. I'm top hand for the LH spread and we were follerin' Holbrook's orders. But we're on our way home now and don't want any more trouble. We're done in an' want no more of this here feudin'.'

'Not me,' one of the men snarled. He gigged his horse out of the line of the other six men and turned towards Matt. 'You are the one who brung all this trouble. I'll jist get rid of you now an' th' trouble'll be over.'

'Cole! Let it be!' Warren yelled, but he was too late. The man gave no other warning, his hand speeding to his sixgun. As it cleared leather Matt gigged his horse sideways, and made his own draw, slower and much behind the other's gun.

Cole's gun blasted and the bullet slapped air beside Matt's ear. Again the man fired, but his horse shied and again he missed. Matt cocked his sixgun and, as it came level, fired one shot. The gun blasted and smoke rolled.

The LH man yelled in pain and then rolled sideways from the saddle as his horse shied and reared. He struck the ground, shivered and relaxed, dead from the bullet that had shattered his heart.

Other LH men made moves toward their guns, but Warren yelled at them. He saw the gun in Matt's hand recocked and poised for another shot.

He did not know the man with Matt, but a wicked Colt .44 was aimed directly at him.

'Hold it! Settle down now. That's enough. There ain't goin' to be no more shootin'.' Warren bulled his horse about and shoved his men back of him. He then faced Matt and Bonner.

'This was none of my orders, Curtis. Let us go back and pick up our wounded and maybe dead from your place and we'll be outta your hair.'

'Not that easy.' Bonner spoke for the first time. 'You can pick up your men, all right. But when you get back to your ranch, you tell your boss, Holbrook, that Todd Bonner, United States Federal Marshal, will be at his ranch early tomorrow, for him to answer for this attack, and some other things.'

Warren nodded. With his men following, he dejectedly turned back to the horse ranch to pick up the crew he had lost in the fight, followed by Matt and Bonner, riding warily behind them.

CHAPTER NINETEEN

The Curtis Horse Ranch men watched silently as Roscoe Warren and his remaining crew snagged wandering horses, belonging to the dead and wounded LH men, then rode dejectedly away.

Matt stood beside Al Rooney.

'Did we take any hits?' he asked quietly. Al shook his head.

'Nope. Nary a man hurt. We had 'em figured out to the last move. It was almost painful to shoot 'em, they were so dumb-founded.' He looked keenly at Matt. 'Frum what one of the LH men told Tip, you potted one of 'em there before you come on in.'

Matt grimaced and then nodded.

'One by the name of Cole just had to try his luck,' he said. He straightened and looked about. 'Nearly daylight,' he said. 'Have Cookie put on a pot of coffee and get all the men into the cook shack. We've got some talking to do.'

The crew was at the tables, sipping coffee

and talking, when Bonner and Matt joined them. As the two sat down and Cookie brought their coffee, the men quieted and looked questioningly at Matt.

'For those of you who haven't met him, this is Federal Marshal Todd Bonner. He came to Rimrock, looking for a man. He has found him. It's Lear Holbrook.' There was nodding and muttering among the men.

'I'm beholden to those of you who stayed back and fought off the LH crew tonight. That should put an end to their trying to take the basin away from us.'

He leaned back and rolled a cigarette, lighted it and drew in a lungful of smoke.

'Come full light, Bonner here is going over to the LH to face Holbrook.' He paused for a moment, then continued: 'I'm going along, just to watch his back.'

There was a stirring among the men, then Tip Wilson spoke up.

'I don't like much throwin' lead at men I've worked with. But if you need someone else along, I'll be willin' to side you.'

Bill Smith spoke up at that point.

'I reckon I can find the time to go with you, boss.'

Bonner was eyeing the younger man thoughtfully.

Matt nodded. 'Thanks to any who want to come along.' He rose and nodded to them. 'Cookie will get breakfast for us all, and then we'll leave.' He nodded to two of the townsmen who were still working on the buildings. 'You just keep on working here. You ain't expected to fight our battles.'

The two men returned his nod, both seeming relieved at his words.

As Matt left the shack, Bill Smith followed him.

'Matt, I have decided to move on. It's gettin' a little cold up here. I think I will move further south for the winter. I'll get my possibles and if you will give me my wages up to now, I'll go with you to Holbrook's. After the affair there is finished, I'll be movin' on.'

Matt eyed the younger man carefully, then nodded.

'You've been a good hand with the hosses, Bill. But if you want to move on, I'll not stand in your way. I'll get your pay up to date, and you can move on, if that's what you want to do.'

Smith nodded. 'Thanks, Matt. Maybe I can help out some at Holbrooks, and then I'll move on.' He turned and went to the corral to rope out his horse.

When Matt left the basin, Al Rooney, Bill Smith and Todd Bonner were with him. At the last minute Cookie came puffing from the corral, where he had saddled his riding-mule. He was carrying his old shotgun in his hand.

'I think I'll jist tag along, Matt. I ain't seen the LH ranch since Holbrook run the fust owner off and took over the spread.'

Matt grimaced and then shrugged.

'Be careful, Cookie. You know good range cooks are hard to come by.'

Cookie glared at him. 'Don't worry, boss. I'll keep up my end.'

As Matt and his companions rode up to the hitchrail in front of the main house of the LH ranch, Holbrook stepped out of the front door and stood on the edge of the veranda. His hands were pushed down, bunched, into the side pockets of his black suit coat.

'None of you has been invited here,' he growled around his cigar. 'None of you is welcome.'

Bonner eyed him levelly.

'Holbrook, I'm here as a federal marshal.'

Holbrook started, his face paling.

'You? A federal marshal? Come all the way from Dakota?'

Bonner nodded. 'Curtis, here, also has a complaint against you for attacking his ranch and firing on his men, unprovoked.'

'Well, just let him complain.' Holbrook leered. 'He's only a town marshal. His jurisdiction runs out at the town limits.' He removed his cigar and spat at the feet of Bonner's horse.

Bonner shook his head. 'He has jurisdiction here, Holbrook. I appointed him deputy United States federal marshal temporarily. Now, I'm arresting you for the murder of Wade Manning, citizen of Sundance County, Dakota Territory. Just come on into Rimrock with me and we'll make all the arrangements to get you back to Sundance.'

Holbrook's face darkened with rage. In a strangled tone he yelled at Bonner.

'You are not taking me any place! If you think you can kill every man on my spread to get me off, then draw your pistol!' He turned his head toward the door he had come through. 'Rainey! Get out here!'

The thin-faced gunslinger, his eyes gleaming with anticipation, stepped through the door. He sidled to the right of Holbrook, his hand hovering, clawlike, over his gun butt.

Roscoe Warren stepped from the bunkhouse, walked to within a few feet of the porch and stood looking at Holbrook.

'Well, don't just stand there, Warren! Get the rest of the crew out here, armed and ready. We'll just finish these three off, bury them, and go back into Rimrock and take over again.'

Warren shook his head. 'It won't be like that, boss. The rest of the crew says they won't fight no more. Too many have got themselves kilt on your say-so, an' nothin' to show fer it. Now, I fight for the spread I work for, so I'll back you. But I'm all you're gettin' out of the crew.'

Al Rooney gigged his horse and moved alongside Curtis.

'Looks like it's the four of us against Holbrook, boss.' He nodded at Lance Rainey. 'I'll take that one,' he said softly.

Matt quietly reached back, drew the ten-gauge shotgun from the saddle sheath and placed it across his lap. He looked at Warren.

'Loyalty is good, Roscoe, but don't be foolish. Step out of this. I have something to show your boss before he starts anything foolish.'

Warren looked at him without speaking, tense, his hand near the butt of his sixgun.

Matt drew a paper from his jacket pocket and looked at Holbrook.

'I know why you wanted the basin so badly, Holbrook. You were told that a railroad spur was putting a track into Rimrock so the ranchers would not have to drive their herds too far for shipment. This letter here will explain something that should let you see that your fight for the basin is futile.' He handed the paper to Holbrook.

'What's this? Some trick to take the basin and keep me out? You already know my feeling about that. Your letter of inheritance is no good. Now, another letter?' He smirked at Matt, but, none the less, unfolded the paper and looked at it.

Holbrook read the paper and paled. His trembling hand shook the letter. He raised his eyes and glared at Matt.

Matt shook his head. 'I know you thought that you would sink a well at that oil seep and sell the oil to the railroad. Then you would have the area surveyed for oil underneath the basin, and become rich, owning all the land where the oil was found.' Matt looked at him with a calm expression.

'There ain't to be a spur built out to Rimrock. You were flimflammed by some fast

talkers. Others too. Then those who persuaded you to invest several thousand dollars
disappeared with the money. Oh, there's oil
there all right. But it will stay where it is until
becomes needed – if ever it is.'

Holbrook let the paper drop to the porch
floor.

'You're lyin'! There's a pool of oil under
the basin that will make what they found
down in Texas look like puddles. I'll take the
basin and I'll be the richest man from here
to St Louis!' In his rage his right hand swept
his coat-tails aside and grasped the sixgun
thrust in his waistband.

Lance Rainey hissed and, crouching, drew
his pistol. He was fast! His hand was a blur
as it sped to his gun. The gun appeared like
magic in his fingers. Cocking as he drew, he
fired. But for all his swiftness, a gun spoke
and a bullet sped through the smoke of his
own gun.

Al Rooney drew, but a gun spoke beside
him. Bill Smith stood, tense, crouched,
holding a smoking sixgun in his hand. On
the porch Rainey staggered and dropped his
pistol. His hands went to his chest, which
was now covered with blood. He looked at
Al Rooney, then fell to the porch and was
still.

Seeing Rooney going into action, Roscoe Warren grimaced, then his hand dropped to his gun butt. He grasped his sixgun, his eyes on the shotgun in Matt's hand, the dark-bore pointed at him. He shook his head, then, grimly and determinedly, he drew his gun and leveled it at Matt.

'No, Warren! Don't do it!' Matt yelled, cocking the hammers of the shotgun. Warren shook his head and bore down upon Matt, firing and cocking the sixgun for another try. The slug from Warren's gun sliced through Matt's hatbrim.

Matt ducked and swung the shotgun around. As Warren's second round was released, he pulled one trigger of the gun. The blast took Warren in the center of his chest, causing his second shot to go high and slamming the man to the ground. He writhed there, twitching, then sighed and became still.

A member of the LH crew burst from the bunkhouse door, gun in hand. Matt saw him, swung about and leveled the shotgun at him. He skidded to a halt, his eyes widened in fright as he saw the shotgun bearing down upon him. He dropped his gun and dived back into the bunkhouse, slamming the door shut behind him.

Holbrook drew his pistol and fired at Bonner. The federal marshal faced him coolly and did not flinch as the slug whined past his head. Again Holbrook fired, his shaking hands causing the round to go wide. Cursing, Holbrook seized the pistol in both hands and aimed deliberately at the lawman, willing his shot to be true.

Only then did Bonner move. His hand slashed to his gun, and as it rose, he fired. A dark hole appeared between Holbrook's eyes. The gun slipped from his limp fingers and he collapsed on the porch. His hands twitched and scrabbled at the floorboards, then relaxed as the darkness of eternity closed about him.

Acrid gun smoke drifted, stinging the eyes and the nostrils of those nearby. The blast and roar of the guns suddenly gone, the silence rang in their ears. Then, slowly, normal sounds crept in. A man shouted from the bunkhouse and opened the door, looking out at the main house. Slowly, one by one, the crew appeared and stood, awkward and wondering, as they viewed the bodies of the three leaders of the spread.

The silence was broken when Bill Smith gigged his horse over beside Matt and looked down at the bodies inert before them.

'They just couldn't let it be, could they,' he said. He looked at Matt. 'I'll be goin' now, Matt. It's been good workin' for you. Thanks very much for everything. Maybe we'll meet up again some day.' He reached over and they shook hands. He reined his horse about.

'So long, Bill. Good luck and if you get back in this neck of the woods, drop in and stay awhile.'

Smith nodded, touching the brim of his hat in a casual salute. Then, turning his horse, he left the area, disappearing down the road leading away from the ranch, and from the vicinity of Rimrock.

'Well, the kid's gone,' Matt murmured to Al Rooney, who had moved over closer to him.

'He called himself Bill Smith. I reckon a man can take whatever moniker he wants.'

Al nodded. 'Names don't mean a lot, no how. Just so you're doin' your job right. An' Bill did his work. He was a good hand with the horses.'

Matt nodded his agreement.

The LH crew stirred and some walked over to the porch to view the bodies of their boss and his protectors. Bonner leaned on his saddle horn and silently observed the men as they surveyed the scene.

'Holbrook was wanted in Sundance, Dakota, for murder,' he told them quietly. 'I'm a federal marshal. Curtis, here, is a temporarily appointed deputy federal marshal. Many of you were involved in attacking his ranch at least twice, so would be liable for arrest. However, you all get your possibles packed, snag your personal horses and leave the area. Those of you not involved can stay on and care for the ranch until further decisions are made. The bank will pay you. I'll see to that. It's up to you.'

One of the older hands looked up at Bonner.

'I haven't had nothin' to do with raidin' Curtis's hoss ranch. Don't believe in such. An' there's four or five of us that'll stay on, iffen y'all make sure these mean cusses Holbrook hired rolls up their blankets an' makes tracks.'

Bonner nodded. 'They'll go, or go to prison. It's up to them.' He looked at Curtis and Matt nodded his agreement. Bonner looked at the man who had just spoken up for the LH crew.

'What is your name, friend?'

'Josh Waters,' the cowhand answered.

220

'Josh, have these bodies taken into Rimrock and turned over to Doctor Marcus. I'll handle it from here on.'

Josh nodded his agreement.

With that, Rooney, Matt and Bonner turned their mounts and rode out of the yard. They left behind them disgruntled hands, men whose lives skirted the edges of the rule of law, and the remains of one whose dreams of power and riches had ended. Violence had acted for the good of law, as so often it did in this part of the territories. Bonner mused as they rode away:

'The law will come, but until then this scene will be played out over and over again.'

Matt and Emmy stood at the edge of the little creek and looked up the slope at the new house. The water murmured quietly under the ice that winter had formed over the surface. She tucked her head against his shoulder.

'Three more days, darling,' she murmured, 'and we will be married in the Rimrock church. It seems so long to wait.' She shivered and reaching up, kissed his cheek.

'I know, honey.' He folded her soft body in his arms. 'Looking at the house there, with everything new in it, I can't help wondering what the years will bring to it.'

'Love, Matt,' she said. Facing him, she placed her palms on his cheeks. 'Full, honest and heart-deep love. As this ranch grows, so will our family–'

'Boys?' he interrupted, with a grin.

'And girls,' she added with a smile.

He held her close. A light snow began to fall. Through the drifting flakes the glow from the window formed a halo and, taking her hands in his, he led her into it and into their future.

The publishers hope that this book has given you enjoyable reading. Large Print Books are especially designed to be as easy to see and hold as possible. If you wish a complete list of our books please ask at your local library or write directly to:

Dales Large Print Books
Magna House, Long Preston,
Skipton, North Yorkshire.
BD23 4ND